GLOW

GLOW

THE FAIRHAVEN CHRONICLES™ BOOK ONE

MARTHA CARR

MICHAEL ANDERLE

DISRUPTIVE IMAGINATION

GLOW TEAM

Thanks to the JIT Readers

Keith Verrett
Kelly ODonnell
Micky Cocker
Alex Wilson
Paul Westman
John Findlay
Kimberly Boyer
Joshua Ahles

If I've missed anyone, please let me know!

Editor
Lynne Stiegler

DEDICATIONS

From Martha

To everyone who still believes in magic and all the possibilities that holds. To all the readers who make this ride so much fun. And to all the readers just like me who create wonder, big and small, every day.

From Michael

To Family, Friends and
Those Who Love
To Read.
May We All Enjoy Grace
To Live The Life We Are
Called.

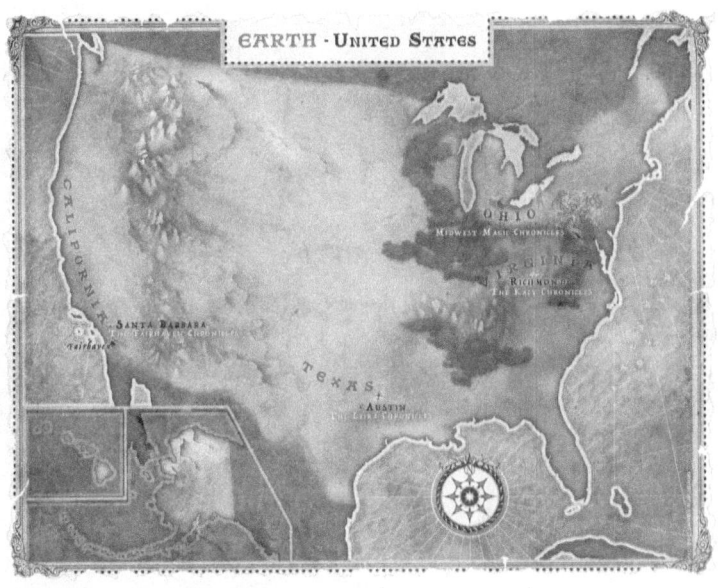

EARTH · UNITED STATES

CALIFORNIA

OHIO
MIDWEST MAGIC CHRONICLES

VIRGINIA
RICHMOND
THE KAZY CHRONICLES

SANTA BARBARA
THE TIERNAN CHRONICLES

TEXAS
AUSTIN
THE LUKA CHRONICLES

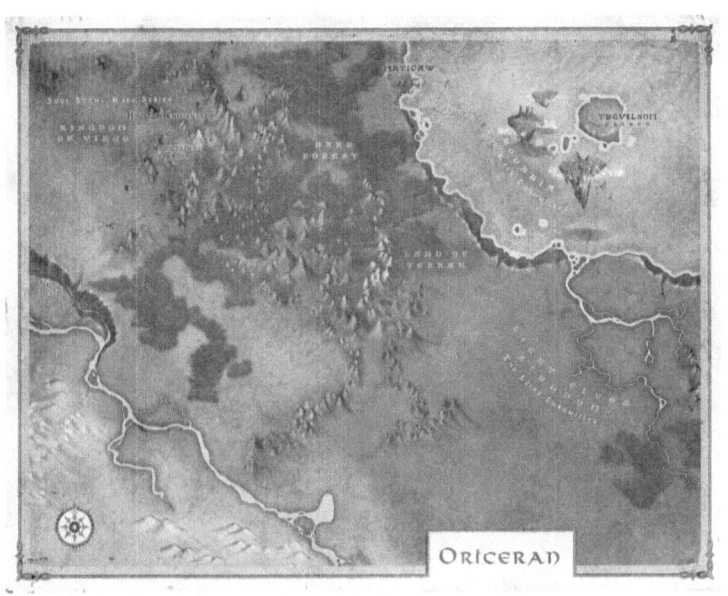

ORICERAN

CHAPTER ONE

A warm breeze rushed over Victoria Brie's face as she leaned her head against the car's doorframe. She smiled as an I-5 onramp whizzed by her, tangles of ivy spilling over the freeway dividers that separated the road from a Seattle suburb. Silky strands of her strawberry hair broke loose from her pony tail and shivered in the wind coming through the open window. Her fingers tapped to the beat of a rock song on the radio as she hummed aimlessly and watched the gray sky.

Home.

Someone slammed on their brakes in front of her. Tires screeched. In the driver's seat, her best friend Audrey Xavier flipped off the driver and peeled into the next lane. "Learn to drive, motherfucker!"

Victoria chuckled. "Girl, you need to chill."

"Are you blind? We nearly got into a wreck."

"It's Seattle. Everyone drives like shit."

Audrey smirked. "Except me, of course."

Victoria laughed. "Of course. You're flawless."

"Damn right I am." She swerved into the next lane with only a foot to spare between her and the car behind them. Victoria rolled her eyes.

Their car rumbled over the bridge between Seattle and Bellevue as Audrey headed to their neighborhood. They'd lived two streets apart their whole lives, which meant free rides for Victoria any time they went anyplace.

"You're going to be at kickboxing tomorrow, right?" Audrey took one of the offramps leading toward their suburb.

"Always."

"Duh, I know you want to. But your arm—"

"Is fine." Victoria rubbed the fist-sized bruise on her bicep that was hidden under her sleeve.

"Maybe lay off sparring for a bit?"

"I'm fine, thanks, *Ma*," Victoria said, rolling her eyes.

Audrey grinned and turned onto Victoria's street. Victoria scanned the houses, all cookie-cutter versions of each other with nothing to differentiate each but the yards and colors of the siding. She loved Seattle, but the suburbs? Not so much.

The car jostled as it pulled into the paved driveway of her parents' two-story home. Aside from the tree in the center of the yard, it looked like every other house on the block, but she didn't care. This one was special. This one was *home*.

The family Jeep sat in the driveway—a pleasant surprise, since her parents were journalists and travel a lot. Looked like she'd get a cooked meal tonight instead of a frozen dinner. She grimaced. *Scratch that*. With her mother's love of too much tabasco, Victoria would probably prefer a frozen dinner.

"See you at school tomorrow," Audrey said.

"You're still okay dropping me off at the grocery store for my shift after classes?"

"Don't I always?" Audrey said with a grin.

"Rub it in, rich girl."

Audrey laughed but dismissed the thought with a wave of her hand. The Xaviers weren't exactly loaded, but at least they could afford to get Audrey a car. No such luck for Victoria. She had to get a job to pay for kickboxing and to save a bit for her own wheels, but she didn't begrudge her bestie. Such was life.

Victoria grabbed her gym bag out of the backseat, heading for the front porch. Eager to get a shower, she jumped the top step as she reached for the door handle.

The front door was ajar, the wood along the frame and lock splintered. It looked as though someone had kicked it in.

Her smile faded. A primal part of her screamed that something was wrong. Her parents never left the door unlocked, much less open.

Throat dry, a slight tremble to her hands, she peeked inside to find the familiar foyer lined with family vacation photos in mismatched frames. On the left, those same glass doors leading to the shared office. Same messy desk littered with papers. On the right, the same doorway into the rarely used dining room. And straight ahead, the same view of the living room.

Except this time, a man's legs protruded around the corner. She recognized those beat-up sneakers.

"Dad!" She ran to him, dropping her gym bag as she got her knees and felt for his pulse. He lay in the hallway leading toward the master bedroom, his face pressed into the drywall. A long streak of blood stained his white button-down, and a few rips in his jeans were covered in blood as well. Thankfully, he was breathing, and his eyes fluttered open as she knelt.

He coughed. Blood splattered against the wall. "You need to go. You need to run, now."

"Dad, what happened?"

He waved away her hands, trying to stand and falling to his knees. "There's no time. You need to get out of here right away."

"I'm not going to leave you, Dad. Where's Mom? What—"

A woman's scream cut through the air. She screamed again, but this time it was cut short. Panic rolled through Victoria like a tsunami hitting a beach.

The primal fight-or-flight urge kicked in, and she was sure as hell going to *fight*.

She bolted to her feet, fists clenched and ready to land a punch on someone's nose or, better yet, groin. When she fought to protect what she loved, she sure as shit didn't play fair.

"C'mon, Dad. We have to find Mom. Let's go!"

Something grabbed her wrist, and she spun on her heel to find her father still on his knees. This wasn't the stoic, strong man who had raised her, taught her to be tough and to walk off her scuffed knees. Instead, she saw a man with one hand on his side as he struggled to breathe, his brows scrunched in pain. To her utter disbelief, tears welled in his eyes. "I failed. I've failed you both. I'm so sorry, Victoria. I'm so sorry."

Jesus. This was way worse than she'd thought. Her breath came in bursts, and the almost uncontrollable urge to run up the steps toward her mother's scream conflicted her. Immobilized, terrified, she searched his face for answers. "Dad, you're not making sense. We have to go help Mom! What if... what if she..."

He pulled Victoria close, cradling her head in his hands as he touched his forehead to hers. "Victoria, you don't have time. Your mom and I, we're goners, but you can still make it out of here alive before he finds you. You can—"

The bottom stair creaked. Victoria spun to find a man, easily six and a half feet tall, leaning against the wall at the bottom of the stairs. He wore a suit, and splotches of fresh red blood splatter stained his white dress shirt. His long black hair was slicked back like a mobster's, and his ears came to a point.

She squinted at his ears, heart hammering in her chest. None of this made sense. Maybe she was losing her mind, or maybe she had passed out after finding the front door ajar.

Had to be. It fucking *had* to be because otherwise, none of it made sense.

The stranger looked her up and down, and for the first time, Victoria noticed blood spatter on his cheeks. "You didn't tell me you had a daughter, old man. Sneaky."

Victoria shuddered at the sound of the man's voice. It was worse than nails on a chalkboard. It had a deep, grating tonality, as if he were drilling a hole in her head with the very sound. His eyes narrowed as she stared at him, the irises flashing red for the briefest of moments.

Paralyzed, Victoria could only stare.

"Victoria, run!" her father shouted.

Something pushed her. She fell forward, landing hard on her shoulder. Her body slid along the hardwood floor from the force. As she finally regained her composure, she had a perfect view of the two men facing off in her living room. The stranger smirked as her father stood and—unbelievably—summoned a sword from thin air.

Victoria's jaw dropped.

The weapon looked like the lovechild of a sword and an axe. The brass hilt curved slightly, and the sharp blade had two curves in it that reminded Victoria of bites out of a sandwich, creating a dizzyingly fierce weapon with three sharp points. It rested easily in her father's hand, although his shoulder dipped a bit as if it were insanely heavy.

Nope, this didn't make sense. Not one bit. Her analytical brain worked overtime trying to rationalize what she had seen, but she couldn't think of any possible way he could make a sword materialize like that, especially not a heavy one. His hand had been empty one second ago, but now a massive broadsword filled it. He lifted his arm and swung at the stranger, who easily ducked out of the way.

Her father grimaced, laser-focused on the attacker with a look of hatred Victoria didn't recognize. This couldn't be her father. Sure, he could be a pain-in-the-ass journalist sometimes when he was asking the wrong people the wrong questions, but he had never before looked like he could kill someone.

And he looked like he was about to massacre this stranger.

Tears long gone from his eyes, her father raised his sword. "Luak, you son of a bitch. If you so much as touched my wife, I swear I'll—"

"Oh, she's dead," Luak answered with a sneer.

Victoria gasped, looking up at the stairs. "Mom!"

"She's next," the stranger said, with a nod to Victoria.

"Over my dead body," her father said.

"That suits me just fine," Luak answered. A spark snapped to life in his palm, flickering like a tiny sun. Within seconds fire erupted across his hands, burning nothing but the air and his hatred.

Victoria gasped.

The men attacked each other, and time slowed. The stranger threw a ball of fire at her dad. The crackle of flames drowned out all other sound. Her father groaned and fell against the wall, sword tilting as he held his side, and Luak raised his hand to strike. Too slow. Her father dove, sword aimed for the stranger's heart, but Luak narrowly avoided the thrust.

Victoria inched toward the kitchen. She needed to get a knife or something—*anything*—that would let her join this fight. But as she prepared to make a run for it, she caught her father's eye. His forehead furrowed, and he sighed. In one horrifying moment she saw his expression shift. He went from furious and vengeful to almost sad. He seemed determined about something, and she had a feeling she wouldn't like what it was.

Oh, God, no.

That was his resigned face, an expression she had seen

only twice before in her life. It marked the moment he gave up on something that meant the world to him.

He lifted his sleeve, which struck her as odd. He always wore long sleeves, even in summer, and he never rolled them up. He joked about always being cold, even when he would sweat.

Now she knew why.

Embedded in his arm was a dagger. The metal had fused with his body, and the intricate curls in the metal blade left small holes through which the wall behind him was visible. Her jaw dropped yet again, and her mind went numb as she tried to process what she was seeing.

He ducked another blow from the stranger, knelt, and slid toward her. Before she could say anything, he grabbed her shoulder and put himself between her and the attacker. The stranger didn't miss a beat. He pulled out a dagger from beneath his suit coat and drove it into her father's chest. Her father shrieked in agony.

"Dad!" she screamed.

A brilliant flash of green light filled the room. A blast of air emanated from her dad, pushing aside everything but the two of them. Couches banged into the walls. Tables flipped. The stranger flew backward, sailing through the front door and onto the porch. Splintered wood ricocheted off the walls and ceiling as the door broke from the force.

Her father collapsed to the ground. Still blinking away the spots in her vision, she stared at her father, grabbing fistfuls of his shirt as she tried desperately to see how he was doing. Blood trickled from the corners of his lips, but he smiled.

"You're going to be okay, Victoria," he said softly.

Crying, throat dry, panicked to hell and back, Victoria could barely think straight. "Dad, stay with me. *Dad!*"

He paused, eyes lingering on hers, mouth trembling a bit. "I love you with all my soul, Baby Bear."

He reached for the dagger embedded in his arm, grimacing as his fingers gingerly pulled the metal from his skin. Blood bubbled from the edges of the artifact as he ripped it out, pooling on the hardwood. He screamed, a bloodcurdling sound that sent shockwaves through Victoria's core. Face contorted in a painful grimace, he pressed the dagger against her own arm. The tip broke the skin and drew blood from her wrist. She flinched, and he collapsed to the ground.

A searing pain unlike anything Victoria had ever experienced in her life burned through her entire body. It was as if she had been set aflame and then thrown in an oven for good measure. She tried to scream, but she couldn't. She tried to move, but she couldn't. Her entire being ached to cry out, to thrash, to get away from the pain, and yet she was immobilized.

Eventually, she became aware that she was leaning on her hands, heaving. The grains of the hardwood came into view bit by bit. Arms shaking, she tried to stand and fell back to her knees. A familiar, eerie voice caught her attention.

"He must have hated you," Luak said.

She narrowed her eyes, seething with disgust at this man who would dare say something so wildly heartless seconds after killing her father. She snarled, her voice nearly a growl. "I'm going to rip you apart, you fucking bastard."

He smirked. "Feisty. I like it."

Dagger aimed at her face, he lunged. Ordinarily Victoria would tap into her two years of kickboxing experience to dodge and turn the knife against him. Any other day, she would have had a clear mind and a strong grip.

But today was no ordinary day.

With her nerves on fire, confused and horrified, Victoria was a slave to her impulses. Her anger and fear blurred into one chaotic emotion she couldn't even name. This lunatic, this murderer, wanted her dead. Her reflexes were wrecked from her ordeal, and she wanted something to cover her, something to protect her from the steel headed for her temple.

As if on command, a shield appeared in her hand. Its shape reminded her of a coat of arms. It weighed down her arm, the bottom edge sinking deep into the hardwood. The floor splintered, and the stranger's knife snapped on the rough iron of her shield.

"What the *hell*?" Astonished, surprised, and freaked right the hell out, Victoria pushed herself against the wall. As quickly as it had come, the shield disappeared into thin air again. Now she was faced with the stranger, who glared at her as if he wanted to rip out her throat with his bare hands.

In her periphery, her father's blood-soaked body lay on the hardwood floor. She pushed herself to her feet, boiling with anger. If this Luak asshole wanted to rip her throat out, he'd have to work for it.

The murderer summoned another spark in his palm, his hand erupting with familiar fire, and she once again lifted her hands to shield her face. And once again, a shield appeared out of thin air. The flame poured past, Victoria safely protected behind the iron shield that had come from nowhere.

And once again, it disappeared just as quickly.

He lifted his hand to attack once more, but the scream of a siren broke through the air. He looked over his shoulder at the gaping hole that was once her front door, tensing. "Let's see how long you last, girl."

"What do you—"

He lifted both hands to the ceiling and flames engulfed his entire body. She screamed as fire funneled off him like a tornado, and heat singed her eyebrows. She coughed, suddenly desperate for air, and crawled away from him. The flames emanating from his body engulfed the house, burning faster than any bonfire she had ever seen. The couch, the table, the ceiling fan—all ablaze.

Through the surging flames, she caught his eye. He sneered and disappeared into the smoke. Something told her he wouldn't be affected, but the heat singed her skin, and she knew she had to get out of here. Desperate, she reached for her father. He didn't move. A knot formed in her throat as she put her finger on his neck to check for a pulse.

Nothing.

Eyes stinging from the smoke and her loss, she headed for the stairwell. She had to look for her mother, had to at least check. But as she started up the steps, a beam fell from the ceiling. It crashed through the stairs, creating a gaping hole that led to the basement.

Coughing, barely able to see, she scanned the upstairs

hallway. Another beam fell, the house burning far too quickly for this to be a normal fire.

The sirens were closer now, the response time too fast for the fire department across town. Someone must have called the cops. The crackling of the flames raged in her ears. She could hear nothing but the snaps and pops of the fire, see nothing but red and orange blurs. Hatred blistered through her, scorching away the last shreds of her self-preservation. She had to get to her mother, had to make sure, had to see for herself.

Her arms were blistered from the heat, and soot coated her skin like clothing. As the smoke filled her lungs, someone grabbed her arms and pulled her backward. She screamed, and the only words she could hear over the roaring fire were, *"Mother! Find my mother!"*

No one answered her.

The heat faded, and her screaming turned to coughing as she fought to breathe. Her eyes stung. She could barely think, barely form words. She fell, hands pressing into the soft, cool grass outside. The blades were like tiny pinpricks of ice against her burned skin as she struggled to draw in air. All she could see was the blistering sun, its golden rays blinding her.

She collapsed onto the grass, cheeks pressed against it as if it were a pillow. Unable to do anything else, she closed her eyes.

Deep in her core, she knew what she had seen.

Magic.

While it should have been mystical and whimsical, in reality it had brought her nothing but pain. Her father had died in her arms. She had heard her mother's last scream.

Her family had been murdered by a stranger, a phantom who looked for all the world like an elf.

Nothing in her old life mattered anymore. Her dead-end job, her dreams, her goals, the money she had saved to buy a car; they were someone else's dreams, traded for a magic dagger that had horrifyingly fused with her body.

And now she had only one purpose: find that stranger, slit his throat, and watch him die. He would pay for what he had done to her, what he had done to her family. He would pay dearly.

She would see to it herself.

Luak watched the melee from a patch of forest not far from the girl's still-burning house. He wanted the dagger her father had given her, and he wanted it *badly.* For now, he had to wait. There were too many witnesses. Even though he could kill everyone here, attacking her now would raise the wrong eyebrows.

For the moment he had to remain unseen, careful and strategic. When the opportunity arose, he would follow her and end what her parents had started.

CHAPTER TWO

Victoria sat on the ambulance's rear bumper, covered by a blanket that she had deliberately arranged to hide the dagger now embedded in her arm. The blistering pain had faded from her burns to the point where she didn't feel like they were there at all. She stared at the asphalt, eyes out of focus as she tried not to think.

A young man in a medic's uniform passed a flashlight over Victoria's eyes. The blinding glare left a streak in her vision, but she didn't bother to follow it. A ringing in her ears kept her from hearing anyone, and she didn't care enough to listen.

A hand reached for her hidden forearm, and she instinctively grabbed the person. Her eyes snapped into focus, and she glared at the medic who had no idea he had nearly touched the strange magical object fused to her body.

"I need to check your arm, okay? I can't see your wounds under that blanket, and you need help," he said in a soothing voice.

Victoria shook her head.

"I know you're in a lot of pain, but I need to be thorough. I have to make sure you're okay. Will you work with me on this?"

"I'm fine," Victoria said.

"You're anything *but* fine," the medic said, a concerned expression passing over his face.

Victoria pulled the blanket tighter to protect whatever it was her father had given her. No one could know she had it. She didn't understand this thing in her body, but it gave her special skills. Skills she figured others might want to take advantage of, or perhaps even take for themselves.

The medic frowned. "Please work with me. I need to check your arm."

Victoria glared. She didn't try to filter herself or temper the expression. Her full rage bled into her face, and she directed it all at him. The medic flinched, eyebrows shooting upward as her expression apparently caught him off-guard.

"I'm *fine*," Victoria repeated, more firmly this time.

He stuttered, fiddling with an opened packet of gauze before finding an excuse to walk away.

This wasn't who Victoria was used to being, and part of her wished she could feel. An icy coldness permeated her, freezing her and taking her over. She wanted to cry, to scream, to ask for help or a hug, but all she could do was stare at the ground. She felt like a statue, heartless and cold.

The cops would question her soon, and she hardly knew what to say. *A fire elf did it, officer. I swear!*

Sure, that would go over well.

As much as she hated to cover for the sick fuck who had killed her parents, she needed to lie if she wanted to avoid being shipped off to a psychiatric ward or, worse, detained as a suspect.

Time was playing tricks on Victoria. It felt as though hours had passed, but the fire still raged. The firemen aimed their hoses at the windows, and jets of water shattered the glass as they tried to tame the blaze. Smoke billowed from the broken glass and holes in the roof. As the flames slowly withdrew, Victoria stepped onto the asphalt and looked at her childhood home.

One of the firemen ran out of the front door, dressed in full garb. A woman lay over his shoulder, her limp head swaying with each of his hurried steps. He set her gently on the front lawn.

Mom.

Victoria scrambled out of the ambulance, screaming her mother's name. Tears blurred her vision. She couldn't think, couldn't speak, couldn't see anything but her mother's body.

Someone grabbed her shoulders and yanked her back. She elbowed the stranger hard, but it didn't seem to faze him. Another pair of hands pulled her back, and before she knew it, she was sitting in the back of a cop car with her nose pressed to the window, tears streaming down her face as she screamed for her mother.

Two medics crowded around the woman's body, their kits lying open on the grass. One held a limp wrist while the other rifled through a bag for something Victoria couldn't see.

Victoria sobbed. She couldn't help it. She lost herself to

tears as her throat burned. The world blurred, and she shrieked as loudly as she could. It was the only way to release the pain, the anguish, the fear, the hatred.

All that fucking *hatred*.

Luak had stolen what was hers. Her family. Her anchor. Her home.

When the sobbing finally began to subside, she found herself pressed against the door as though she had been trying to push through it. She could barely breathe through the knot in her throat, but her vision began to clear. There were now four medics on the grass surrounding *two* bodies.

Dad.

The young man who had been helping Victoria earlier rubbed his eyes, his shoulders drooping as he knelt beside her mother's body. He sighed and closed his medical kit. With a gesture of his finger, another medic lifted a sheet over Victoria's mother's body. A moment later, a second sheet covered her father.

No.

God, no!

Every shred of self-restraint dissolved in that second. The entire day caught up with her, all her panic and fear slamming her in the chest at once. Her destroyed home. The dagger in her arm. The elf. Magic. Her father fighting to save them. Her mother's scream. A stranger in her house.

It was too much. She couldn't take it anymore.

Victoria pressed her palms against the window again and screamed. It was an unhinged wail from the deepest part of her soul, and it swallowed every emotion until she could feel only a vast void. Even then she didn't stop. She couldn't. Her agony consumed her, and she screamed until her voice died in her throat.

Victoria sat on the ambulance's bumper again, staring at the asphalt with no concept of time or feeling. After she had lost her voice in the back of the cop car, it had been as though a door slammed on her emotions. The numbness ate her alive. She couldn't cry anymore, and she wanted nothing more than to curl in a ball and hide.

A cop had finally let her out of the car when she stopped screaming and calmed down, but in reality she simply didn't have any energy left to fight. The firemen had finally tamed the blaze, and black char marks decorated the siding above every window. A breeze kicked up, taking soot and ash with it.

Her throat still ached from screaming, but she savored the pain. As the minutes wore on, it was all she could feel: no sadness, no hatred, no joy. Only the dull ache in her throat, and an overwhelming emotional numbness.

"Victoria!" someone shouted. A familiar voice. A girl's voice, someone she had known her whole life.

She raised her head, scanning the sea of police and onlookers, and a sliver of gratitude crept into her numb heart. "Audrey?"

Sure enough, a familiar brunette dodged through the onlookers and ducked under the yellow caution tape. A policeman tried to usher her back, but Victoria leapt to her feet and pulled Audrey into a hug before he could manage to shoo her away. Victoria squeezed her friend so tightly she heard Audrey gasp for air. Her childhood friend squeezed back, her tears soaking Victoria's shirt.

Victoria suddenly hated herself even more. Her friend could cry, but Victoria's hatred drowned out her sadness. A lust for revenge and justice consumed her like the fire had consumed her house. Her nails dug into Audrey's shirt as she frowned. Victoria had seen the face of the man who killed her parents, and she would do everything in her power to destroy him.

Luak scowled, surveying the scene as more and more worthless humans mobbed the burnt home. He did his best to keep his eye on the girl, but even her light-red hair became harder and harder to keep track of in the sea of bobbing heads and flashing lights.

At first she had been by an ambulance, and then she had rushed toward the sea of onlookers. She blended with the crowd, perhaps on purpose, until he lost sight of her completely.

He had somehow lost her.

A burning sensation crept down his back. He cursed under his breath, scratching at the metal artifact infused between his shoulder blades just as the dagger had been infused in the girl's father. His artifact hummed, vibrating within him, as angry as he was that she had escaped. He wished his master had given him one of the artifacts that could track other artifacts, but it didn't matter. Not really. He was his master's best hunter, and he had killed more of the artifact hosts than anyone else.

He would find this girl. It was only a matter of time.

Unsure of where else to go, Victoria retreated through the forest behind her destroyed home until she found the treehouse she and Audrey had shared as children. She climbed the rickety ladder and laid on the planks, not even caring if they fell to the ground under her weight. These old boards were accustomed to eleven-year-olds, not fully grown high school seniors.

Audrey followed suit, squatting as she leaned against the trunk of the tree that protruded through the middle of their old refuge. They sat in silence, Audrey occasionally eyeing Victoria.

Victoria knew what was coming. Questions. Lots of questions. But Victoria had questions of her own, and she had no idea how to get answers.

"You look scary as fuck, Victoria," Audrey said.

Victoria quirked an eyebrow, finally meeting her friend's eye.

Audrey nodded. "You look like you're about to kill someone."

"I am," she said, her voice nothing more than a hoarse whisper from all the screaming earlier.

"Come on, now. The fire department said it was probably an accident. You don't need to go after any homebuilders or—"

"The fire didn't kill them. A man did."

A look of horror spread across Audrey's face. She set a hand on her chest, mouth gaping.

Victoria sat up and lifted the blanket that was still around her shoulders to reveal her soot-covered arm and the glittering metal of the dagger embedded in her skin.

Audrey cussed loudly and jumped to her feet, the tree-house shuddering under the sudden jolt. "What the hell is that?"

"I have no idea, Audrey, but my dad had it first. It—it does things, Audrey. It summons things."

Eyes wide, Audrey watched Victoria, squinting as if she didn't know what to believe. "You're not making any sense."

"Magic, Audrey. This thing is magic."

Audrey glanced from Victoria to the metal dagger and back. "I confess this is weird, but I think you maybe inhaled too much smoke. Magic isn't real."

Victoria huffed, her patience altogether gone. She had to show Audrey what she meant, knowing nothing she said would make a difference until she could summon something to prove her claim. The problem? She couldn't control it. At all.

Frustrated, angry, still hurt, and incredibly pissed off, Victoria stood, voice thick with emotion. "You didn't see what I saw, Audrey. You didn't see the fire shooting out of that guy, you didn't see the flames that burned so much faster than they should have. You didn't see my dad..."

Just like that, Victoria was back in the living room, her dad's blood-soaked body collapsed on the living room floor. The knot caught in her throat once more, and she wished she could hide.

As if on cue, the shield appeared in her hand. Seconds later, it crashed to the ground and took her with it. It embedded itself into the wooden planks, causing the tree-house to shake violently. Several boards fell off, revealing the ground below.

"Shit!" Audrey and Victoria said in unison.

Victoria was struggling to pull it out of the floor when the shield disappeared as quickly as it had come. She fell face-first onto the splintered boards and groaned, both frustrated and disgusted with this new thing in her body that she didn't understand.

"Holy fuck!" Audrey ran her hands through her hair one after the other as she paced the rickety treehouse. Eyes wide, mouth gaping, she never stopped staring at the magical dagger.

Victoria lifted her hands, patting the air between her and Audrey in an attempt to calm her down. "Audrey—"

"What the fuck?"

"Audrey, take a—"

Audrey made a gesture that looked something like panic-induced jazz-hands. "It just—*boom*—and then—what the *fuck*, Victoria? Was that a shield?"

"Girl, I know. Deep breaths. I'll tell you what happened, but you need to calm down."

Audrey inhaled breath after breath, wheezing a little. Shoulders heaving, brows raised almost to her hairline, she set her hands on her hips and simply stared at the dagger. "You have about ten seconds to explain what the hell is going on."

Victoria squinched her eyes together as a fresh wave of anger boiled to the surface. "The guy who killed my parents is named Luak, and he wants this dagger in my arm. He killed my dad for it, and he said he was going to come for me next. But you know what? He won't have a chance. I'm going to obliterate him, Audrey. There won't be anything left of him to recognize when I'm done."

This wasn't like anything Victoria had ever said or promised before, but deep in her soul she knew it was more than just talk. It was a vow, one she would see through to the bitter end.

"Goddamn," Audrey mumbled.

"*What.*" Victoria had meant for it to be a question, but in her anger, she barked the word as though it were a command.

"You're scary as fuck right now, you know that?"

Victoria chanced a look at Audrey, who leaned against the far corner of the shaking treehouse. Hand on her heart, Audrey gave Victoria a once-over. Her expression slowly shifted, blurring with too many emotions for Victoria to name. She studied her lifelong friend, doing her best to gauge Audrey's reaction. She expected concern, maybe confusion or even fear.

Instead, true to her amazing friend's nature, Audrey grinned. "What, do you think I'm going to stop you? *Hell,* no. You're the one who talks me out of doing stupid shit, not the other way around. Let's get justice."

Victoria couldn't smile, but she managed a small smirk. It was the best she could do, all things considered.

Audrey nodded at the dagger in Victoria's arm. "What is that thing? How do you use it?"

Victoria shook her head. "I haven't the faintest idea. So far it does what it wants."

Truth be told, this was daunting as hell. She knew nothing about magic, who this guy Luak was, or what was in her arm. Between the magic and the murders, it was almost too immense to fully fathom what she had gotten herself into. However, her journalist parents had taught her one very useful technique for handling the impossible: find the right sources and ask questions until you get answers.

There was information to gather, and her parents had taught her how to hunt for it. She wasn't going to jump into the fight without facts. Though Victoria had always been a bit of a lone wolf, her parents had contacts all over the globe. It put her at a disadvantage to not have access to those people, but she would figure it out. When the time came, she would have exactly what she needed to destroy the man who had tried to kill her.

Audrey lifted a fist, but hesitated for a second before offering it. "I won't lie to you, Victoria, I'm still freaked out by all this. But I know you, I trust you, and I'm with you to the end."

Victoria bumped her fist against Audrey's, the barest smile on her lips. "To the end."

CHAPTER THREE

Several days after the fire Victoria stood in front of her parents' closed caskets with a lump in her throat. Her hands hovered over the wood, and in the hushed funeral parlor, she felt eyes on the back of her neck. Dozens of people had turned out for her parents' memorial service, but she didn't care. She had been waiting for this moment, aching to be close to them again.

Her lips quivered, throat aching, but the tears didn't come.

A picture of her mother smiling in her garden had been placed above the casket on the left, and above the casket on her right was a large portrait of her father writing at his desk. They each beamed at the camera, full of life and joy Victoria hadn't felt since the fire.

It wasn't smart to be here. With Luak after her, she should have run away. She should have taken off to get her questions answered and never paused for even a moment's rest.

But she hadn't been able to.

Everything had hinged on the funeral, as it was her only chance to say goodbye. Evil murderer or no, she wouldn't have missed this for the world. In the end, it wasn't *how* Luak had destroyed her life that mattered; it was what he had taken from her.

Family.

These past few days, Victoria hadn't left Audrey's guest room. She had laid in bed, sometimes staring at the wall, sometimes tossing and turning as she had nightmares filled with magical fire, murderous elves, and her mother's screams.

Suffice it to say, Victoria didn't sleep well.

Thankfully, the coroner, fire department, and police department worked double-time to close the investigation and get her parents cleared for a funeral. The fire was deemed an accident, and Victoria never had to tell the truth to anyone but Audrey.

Her fingertips brushed the wood of her father's casket, and a jolt of sadness rushed through her like lightning. Bit by bit, the numbness began to erode. She sniffled, aching to hug him again, to hear him call her his little girl one more time.

Her face contorted as the tears finally burned in her eyes.

She set her left palm against her mother's casket, the chilly wood almost like cold skin. She imagined the woman lying beneath the lid, the woman who had nursed her through heartache and loss, who would run her fingers through Victoria's hair to soothe her when she was sad.

How she longed for that now.

Victoria didn't hold back. The sobs shook her body, and she surrendered to them. This wasn't the closure she had been expecting. The pain only worsened with each tear. Her chest only ached *more.* Her anger only boiled *hotter.* Deep down, she had hoped that the goodbye would heal at least one aching part of her heart, but it had only ripped her to shreds—again.

She wished she were alone. She hated that the guests who had come to the funeral could see this, but none of them mattered anymore.

Well, none but Audrey.

Luak wanted Victoria dead, which meant Audrey was in danger too. Anyone near Victoria could die. *Would* die.

Victoria looked over her shoulder to find her friend sitting in the front row, biting her lip as dozens of attendees in dark colors pretended not to look. Audrey stood, hands clasped in front of her as a concerned expression crossed her face.

To the end.

A warm ray of gratitude snaked through Victoria's all-consuming sadness. At least she had Audrey. She didn't have to face this alone.

She knelt beside the caskets, trying her best to say goodbye. The word caught on her tongue for what felt like ages until she gave up trying to say it. The tears stopped, and her hatred flared again.

"I'll kill him, I promise," she whispered instead to the caskets. It was a vow she would keep, even if it cost her life.

The next day Audrey palmed the wheel as she pulled out of her suburb onto the freeway. Victoria sat in the passenger's seat, shoulders slumped as she stared out the window.

Victoria usually had an appreciative grin on her face as she watched the city blur by. Between the ivy growing on the overpasses and the way light glimmered on the surface of Lake Washington, there was always something for her to love on their drives.

Not today.

The gray overcast sky seemed to reflect Victoria's mood. Almost no light could penetrate the cloud cover, which made it feel as if the sun would set any second even though it was only nine-thirty in the morning.

Victoria had continued to live in her friend's guest room, borrowing Audrey's clothes and mostly staying in bed.

"That's it!" Audrey snapped. She moved into the far-right lane and took the first exit.

"What are you doing? The lawyer's office is downtown," Victoria said, voice still a bit hoarse.

"Yeah, and he can wait."

"Audrey, this is important. When he pulled me aside after the funeral yesterday, he said he had to speak to me immediately. He said it was urgent, that Mom and Dad—" Her voice broke, and she stared once more out the window.

Audrey's grip tightened on the wheel. "Your parents' lawyer wants you in his office less than twenty-four hours after the funeral to talk about something urgent in their will. That's not weird to you?"

"Don't..." Victoria sniffled, and Audrey knew what her friend had meant to say.

Don't talk about them. It's still too raw.

Audrey didn't know much about death or lawyers, but her parents had complained about how it had taken ages to get through the legal system after her grandmother died. The process took time. It didn't happen overnight.

Between that and the dagger embedded in Victoria's arm, something smelled rotten about this whole affair.

Victoria cleared her throat. "We have to—"

"He can wait. You need a break from death and lawyers and funerals and this magic bullshit that's in your arm. We're going to the bridge."

Victoria frowned for a second, eyes shifting out of focus until it clicked for her. "What, the one we snuck underneath when we were kids?"

"Bingo."

The car screeched a little as Audrey took a curve too fast, careening toward the overpass that would take them to their childhood haunt. It didn't take long to get there. Soon enough she shifted into park and stepped onto the muddy embankment.

A light chill bit her skin, and she looked forward to the gray skies clearing up later in the day. It was summer, damn it. They deserved what little sun the Pacific Northwest could offer.

Audrey led the way down the muddy slope, skidding here and there. Following behind her, Victoria slipped in the mud and yelped as her ass landed hard on the ground.

For a second they simply stared at each other. Then, as

if on cue, they burst out laughing. Victoria shook out her mud-covered hands. "I look like I fell in a pile of shit."

"C'mon." Audrey offered her hand, and Victoria took it. They inched down the rest of the bank, taking a bit more care this time. Below, the gentle river wandered underneath the bridge, gurgling and bubbling on occasion. Once at the bottom Audrey ran under the bridge and picked up a rock, barely taking a second to aim before she threw it toward a metal plate bolted to the top of the arch. It missed by inches.

Being down here always did a funny thing for Audrey: it softened her heart. Down here, she could laugh harder and relax more deeply. It was as if by merely walking under the bridge, she was eleven again. The world and its problems faded until there was nothing left but her, her best friend, and the kind of perfect happiness that came with being a kid.

"I had forgotten how much I loved this place," Victoria said, grabbing a rock. She chucked it at the metal plate, and hers hit. A resounding metal hum reverberated through the underpass. The vibration struck Audrey deep in her core even as ripples formed on the water.

"Ha! First try!" Victoria did a muddy moon-dance across the pebbles.

"Lucky shot."

"*Phht.* It's because I'm amazing."

Audrey chuckled and threw another rock, missing the plate by several yards.

"Nice throw," Victoria said with a wink.

"Hush, you."

Victoria sighed happily. "What is it about this place? It's just a bridge, but it's perfect."

Audrey shrugged and sat on the rocky embankment. "It's our childhood. We had some of the best summers ever down here, throwing shit into the water."

Victoria chuckled. "Remember when I accidentally pushed you in and you had to walk back home with your feet squishing on the pavement?"

Audrey rolled her eyes. "Yeah, 'accidentally' my ass."

With a chuckle, Victoria settled in next to her, elbows on her knees as they surveyed the gentle river before them. "Maybe we should just stay down here."

"Sure. We can live off bugs. You like the taste of raw beetles, right? Yum!"

"Shut up." Victoria nudged Audrey's shoulder.

"Sounds nice though, doesn't it? Run away from everything to a place where we're safe, no one's dead, and life is perfect?"

Victoria's smile fell and she stared into the water. "I don't want to run away. I just want a minute of quiet to think."

"Take as many as you need."

They sat together in silence, only the burbling water keeping them company. Audrey stretched out on the bank, the rocks digging into her back like a shitty massage chair. Hands behind her head, she stared at the top of the bridge and let her mind wander to everything and nothing in particular.

"Thank you, Audrey," Victoria eventually said.

"It was nothing."

"It was. This helped me a lot. We should get going, but Audrey... Thank you."

Audrey pulled her into a hug. "Any time."

An hour and a change of clothes later Audrey sat in a lawyer's lobby, twirling her thumbs as she and Victoria waited to be called into his office almost two hours after they had been scheduled to arrive. Audrey had lent Victoria some jeans and a tee, but they would need to go shopping since everything Victoria owned had been burnt to a crisp.

It was the most stereotypical lobby she had ever seen in her life. A row of plush black chairs sat along the walls on either side of the door, and a stuffy middle-aged receptionist sat at her desk facing them. Her half-moon glasses were balanced on the end of her nose as she read a musty old novel with no dust jacket. Audrey could almost smell the moth balls from here. Classical music played softly overhead, and the secretary licked her fingers before turning a page in her book. Audrey grimaced.

Victoria sat quietly beside her, eyes out of focus and arms crossed as she stared at the floor with an expression bordering on hatred. This wasn't like her at all. Audrey desperately wished she could help Victoria in some way, but the girl had barely spoken and hadn't eaten anything since yesterday. "The Incident," as Audrey had taken to calling it for the sake of their sanity, had all but shut Victoria up. Usually Victoria was the happy, bubbly one. In any other circumstances she would be chatting up the secretary and learning her favorite kind of cake, because that was just the kind of person Victoria liked to be. She cared about that stupid shit. Audrey was the quiet, brooding asshole who kept people from taking advantage of her friend. They balanced each other. Audrey wasn't used to being the comforting one.

The lawyer's office door opened, and he gestured Victoria in. He didn't bother looking at Audrey, but that wasn't uncommon. Next to Victoria, even a supermodel would look a little boring. Audrey didn't love it, but she often played second fiddle. She stood anyway.

"Miss Brie only, please," the lawyer said.

"Audrey comes," Victoria said, voice firm.

The lawyer frowned, the wrinkles in his cheeks and chin doubling. "I'm afraid I must insist—"

Victoria shook her head. "Audrey is the only family I have left. She's coming. Get on with it."

Audrey smiled with gratitude. Victoria always had her back, no matter what, no matter who was involved. True, they weren't related in any way, but they had been friends since kindergarten. Victoria really *was* family, as much as a friend could be. But she wasn't used to hearing her friend be so curt and commanding. Being the pushy asshole was Audrey's job.

He sighed, apparently resigned, and gestured for them to enter. As the door closed behind them, they sat in the two chairs in front of a painfully neat desk. Aside from a pen, only a dark green folder lay on its surface, Victoria's name written in silver Sharpie on the front. Victoria gestured to it. "I don't want what remains of the house. Sell the land, give it to charity—I don't care. I'm never going back there."

"Understandable," the lawyer said with a nod. "First of all, I'm sorry for your loss, Miss Brie. I always enjoyed speaking with your parents, even outside the office."

Victoria sat back in her seat, nodding once in thanks.

"Let me go ahead and break everything down. For starters, there was a sizable insurance policy on the house. We can collect that in lieu of rebuilding and sell the land to a developer. Will that work for you?"

Victoria nodded.

"I assume you want to sign off on whomever I choose?"

"I don't care at all."

The lawyer huffed, taking off his glasses and cleaning them with a cloth as he spoke. "Miss Brie, this was your childhood home, wasn't it? I would hate for you to make a choice you would regret. I know you're in pain, and I know I'm putting you in a difficult position. I regret that we must do this so soon after your parents—"

Victoria cleared her throat, cutting him off. Audrey set a hand on Victoria's long sleeve shirt as a sign of comfort, the hard metal of the magical dagger under her fingertips. Victoria tensed but allowed it. It was hot as hell today, a rare blessing in the Pacific Northwest, but Audrey didn't blame Victoria for hiding that thing. Audrey couldn't help herself; she shuddered at the thought of having something like that in her.

"The point is," the lawyer continued, "there are options. We could always rebuild the house, sell it later if you decide that's still what you want."

Victoria narrowed her eyes. "You have kids?"

He squinted, apparently as confused as Audrey at the question. "Yes."

"Could you set foot in a house again if the living room reminded you of the time you saw one of your children die in your arms?"

The lawyer's jaw tensed. "No, I suppose not."

"It's not much different for me. Sell the house, the land, and everything that survived the fire."

He nodded and rifled through more of the papers in the folder. "That said, your parents had several active insurance policies. Namely, life insurance. They named you as the beneficiary, of course, which leaves you with a net worth of over five million dollars."

"Holy shit," Audrey said under her breath.

The lawyer glared at her, but eventually nodded. "It's a substantial amount, I agree."

Victoria, however, didn't bat an eye. She leaned back in her chair, her left thumb rubbing the shirt sleeve which covered the dagger embedded in her arm.

The lawyer skimmed the final papers in the stack. "Nearly all of your parents' estate comes from the insurance policies. It may take a little while for us to collect them, but you will have more than enough to keep you comfortable for the rest of your life if you're frugal with it."

Audrey frowned, her mind wandering to the dagger in Victoria's arm. Apparently, it had first been embedded in her father, which meant Victoria's parents must have gone down one hell of a deep rabbit hole to find it. They had found something dark, something that could get them killed. From the looks of these insurance policies, they probably knew they wouldn't survive.

But if that were the case, it didn't make sense for Victoria's father to pass the torch to Victoria, his only child. If it had been Audrey, she would've hidden it, done anything to keep Victoria from being connected to something that might kill her. That was what family was supposed to do—protect each other. She gritted her teeth, brimming with resentment on her friend's behalf.

The lawyer rifled through his desk drawer. "There's also this—the key to a safe deposit box at the bank four blocks down. They didn't tell me what's in it. I'm simply supposed to give this to you last."

Victoria took the key, examining it in silence. As it twirled in Victoria's hand, Audrey caught a number in black writing on its flat, round face:

153

Audrey bit her lip, waiting for her friend to say something, anything, but it didn't seem like that would happen.

"Thank you," Audrey said, standing.

The lawyer nodded and gestured to the door. "If you have any questions, Victoria, you have only to give me a call. You ladies have a nice day."

A humorless chuckle escaped Victoria. "Yeah, right."

As they walked through the lobby and out into the hall of the shared office building, they passed a row of windows facing the street below. Several shops squeezed together along the historic road, their signs swinging in the gentle breeze of the summer day. A tailor. A hardware store. A diner.

Victoria paused, her gaze lingering out the window. "Mom used to take me to that diner. We would get a hot fudge sundae and share it."

Audrey set a hand on Victoria's shoulder. "Good, because I could go for some ice cream right now."

"You hate ice cream. You used to say it's what weak people eat when they can't handle whiskey."

"True, but I'm worried about you, and ice cream usually cheers you up. Let's go."

Audrey munched on a fry while she watched the brooding Victoria stab her spoon into the sundae as it melted from neglect. She hadn't even taken a bite yet. Plates clinked and coffee was poured in the bustling diner. The mumble of two dozen conversations filled the air.

"I think I'm broken, Audrey," Victoria said.

Audrey tossed her half-eaten french fry onto her plate and leaned her elbows on the table, doing her best to give Victoria an encouraging look. It probably wasn't working, but she didn't care. She was really worried about her friend. "Victoria, stop this shit. Right now."

"What?" Victoria snapped her head up, eyes wide with apparent surprise. Good. At least Audrey had her attention.

"I'm the asshole. You're the fun one. That's how this works. And come on, girl. You're not broken. You're hurt. You're grieving. It's called being normal."

Victoria pointed to the dagger hidden by her long-sleeved shirt. Her voice came out in a harsh whisper. "This isn't normal!"

"I—granted, no, that's weird as hell."

"And I can't cry. Not since I saw their bodies."

"I know, but—"

"No, you don't understand. Not even a little. All I can think about is killing that guy. Slitting his throat and ripping him open with my bare hands. This isn't like me. I don't even recognize myself."

The man behind her stiffened and looked over his shoulder, a combination of bewilderment and fear on his face.

"Not your convo, buddy," Audrey said.

He caught her eye and turned sharply back to his food.

Audrey leaned toward Victoria and pushed the melting ice cream aside. Honestly, she didn't know what to say. "You just need time, V."

"Maybe," Victoria muttered.

"Time," Audrey continued, "and revenge."

Victoria leaned in, face stoic and intense, her voice a whisper. "I've never killed anyone before, but I'm not kidding when I say I'll kill this man. He murdered my mother and father. He took everything from me. I don't care if I'm only eighteen. I will not hesitate to obliterate this guy. Are you sure you want to see that?"

Audrey nodded, slowly at first. "I know you're hurt, and I know you're serious. I don't blame you. This bastard killed your parents right in front of you. I would want justice, too."

Victoria scoffed. "Me saying all this doesn't freak you out?"

Audrey shrugged. "I love you, idiot. Of course I'm going to help you through this."

That got a small smile out of Victoria, at least. "We just need someone to point us in the right direction, as Dad would say."

"I think someone already did," Audrey said, pointing to the key in Victoria's pocket.

Victoria nodded. "You think they left me answers? Some idea of what we're really up against?"

"If I know your parents? All that and more."

Victoria pulled the key out of her pocket, studying it once more in the sunlight coming into the diner window. "Let's not waste any time, then."

CHAPTER FOUR

For the first time since the fire, Victoria felt excited. She had to actively keep herself from pushing past the bank manager and finding the damn safe deposit box herself.

The manager's high heels clacked on the tile floor, the clicks echoing in the quiet space. There wasn't even bland, outdated music playing—only silence and the incessant tapping of the woman's shoes.

She turned a corner, leading them toward the open vault. The vault door sat open, the three-foot-thick steel almost as intimidating as the second barred door separating the hallway from the interior. Victoria marveled at the depth of the vault's walls as she entered—if the door shut on them, they would be screwed.

Inside, the vault was lined with safe deposit boxes about as wide as a hardcover book, all of them adorned with gold locks and gilded numbers.

"Ah, here we go," the manager said, tapping one of the boxes.

Victoria studied the number:

153

The bank manager inserted Victoria's key and her own and twisted them both in their respective locks. With a tiny creak, the squat door opened, and she slid out a thin box the size of a textbook. Victoria nearly protested—this is something she wanted to examine in private. Heels clacking once more over the vault floor, the manager led them into the hallway again and closed the metal gate behind them.

A little confused, Victoria followed with Audrey in tow as the woman led them to a tiny room across the hall. Aside from the pale wood of the round table and the two bland chairs, the room had only florescent light. Not even a window.

The manager set the box on the table and smiled. "We like to give our clients a bit of privacy while they deal with their things. When you're done, just ring the bell here." She pointed to a little buzzer in the wall, not unlike a doorbell. "Do you need anything else?"

"No, thank you," Victoria said with a forced smile.

"I'll leave you to it, then," the woman said, handing over Victoria's key. Her heels tapped on the floor as she returned to the hallway, and the door clicked shut.

Victoria caught Audrey's eye as she readied herself to open the box. "Now or never."

Audrey nodded. "I hope this has some answers."

No kidding. "Me, too."

The top of the box popped upward as if it were on a spring, and she lifted it the rest of the way to reveal the box's contents.

A gun.

"Shit," she hissed. A pistol not unlike the ones she saw in action movies lay in the deposit box, a full clip of bullets next to it. She lowered the lid and looked around for a camera or something that might be recording them.

"A gun?" Audrey leaned in, her voice a whisper as she set a hand on the top of the box as well.

Fighting the panic and nerves fluttering in her chest, Victoria did her best to keep her voice low. "What the hell did my parents get into?"

Audrey gritted her teeth and shook her head, apparently as mystified as Victoria.

Tenderly, gingerly, Victoria peeked underneath the lid again. The gun hadn't budged. It must have been heavy.

A gun. Jesus.

Beside the pistol was an emerald-green pouch with gold drawstrings. She slipped it out, half-expecting a grenade based on the box's contents so far. Instead, though, she found tiny crystals—hundreds of them. They glittered in the artificial light, glowing faintly green. She smiled, grateful that something beautiful was beside something so deadly.

At the bottom of the box was a white spiral notebook with a single word scribbled on the front in black Sharpie:

Oriceran

"I feel like I'm in a Jason Bourne novel," Audrey muttered under her breath. "Cryptic clues left in a safe deposit box. A gun. Next thing you know someone is going to burst in here, bullets flying."

"Well, don't jinx it," Victoria said, rolling her eyes.

She picked up the spiral notebook, and a simple white

envelope fell to the tiled floor. Her name had been written on the front in her father's handwriting.

Her throat caught, and she brushed her thumb across the letters. She paused, savoring something familiar in a sea of strange.

Audrey patted her shoulder, squeezing lightly for comfort. They had known each other so long that Audrey didn't even need to say anything.

It's okay, the gesture said.

With a deep breath, Victoria ripped open the envelope to find a single piece of paper covered in blue ink. Her father's familiar tight handwriting covered the page.

Darling Victoria—

If you are reading this, I'm dead. I'm sorry I left you to face this alone.

The writer in me hates those words because they don't do the truth any justice. I never thought I would have to write a letter to explain things to you once I had passed, except maybe a few times in Afghanistan when I was covering the war and wasn't sure if I would make it home.

But this, Victoria, is worse than war.

There's so much more to our world than I ever thought possible. Your mother and I have discovered only a small part of it, and we wanted to protect you from it. But as you've probably guessed by now, we didn't have so much life insurance out of luck. We figured something would happen to us, and we knew in the long run we wouldn't be able to stop the people coming after us from coming after you. We simply wanted to give you a proper childhood and a chance to live a normal life before you were inevitably ripped from it.

In the spiral book you'll find our notes, everything we've learned so far about the truth hidden right beneath our noses. There are all sorts of creatures, Victoria, all sorts of, well, there's nothing else to call it but magic.

A simple letter won't do it justice, which is why we gave you the spiral notebook. Low tech, I know, but we didn't want anyone to hack us. But know this: we love you. We love you completely, and we're sorry for any way we have failed you. Part of me wanted to train you the moment your mother and I discovered this other world, this place called Oriceran, but you were so young. I was torn between keeping you safe and making you aware of the truth.

I hope I didn't fail you.

I can tell you that if your mother and I are gone, you're no longer safe here. As soon as you can, you need to go to Santa Barbara. I know that California is quite a drive, but there is a hidden city there called Fairhaven. Directions are in the notebook. Go there and find a man named Fyrn Folly. He can answer all your questions, and he'll help you figure out what to do next. He will keep you safe.

With all my love,

Dad

Doing her best to fight back the lump in her throat, Victoria set the letter on the table and picked up the spiral notebook, fingers brushing the black Sharpie on the front.

Oriceran

She hovered over the strange word, not even sure how to pronounce it. But it was more than a word, wasn't it? It was a whole world, the answer she had been looking for. She thumbed through the notebook, its pages alternating between her father's and her mother's handwriting. There were entries with words she didn't understand and pictures that didn't make sense.

She paused on one picture of her parents posing with a seven-foot tall creature. It had thick arms, not unlike tree trunks, and a body as round as a barrel. Its brown skin was covered in boils and warts, and it grinned with a crooked smile full of teeth that didn't quite match up. One long tooth protruded over its lips, nearly touching its nose.

If Victoria hadn't seen fire shoot from the elf's hand, hadn't experienced a shield appearing out of nowhere, she might've thought it was a wax figurine, albeit a really, really good one. But deep in her soul, she knew better. This was a real creature, something magical.

Something she needed to see for herself.

She stumbled across a page with the title "Fairhaven" and skimmed it for answers. There was a bridge in Santa Barbara she needed to go to with a symbol she needed to press, and stairs would appear.

Jesus, what next? A broom and an invitation to Hogwarts?

She dropped the spiral notebook on the table, rubbing her temples as she fought to process the information crashing over her. It was almost too much, but her parents had taught her enough about journalism and investigative reporting to make it through. She simply needed a break, a moment to breathe. She would pick up the book again later.

"Fuck," Audrey said under her breath. She set the letter on the table, eyeing Victoria with a combination of concern and fear.

But Victoria wasn't afraid. Overwhelmed? Sure. A little nervous? Absolutely. But afraid? Not a snowball's chance in hell. This was exactly what she needed: answers, a direction, something to do.

She would learn everything there was to learn about this world, about its creatures, and about this monster named Luak. And when she had learned all there was to learn, she would use her new knowledge to make Luak pay for everything he had taken from her.

"Guess we're going on a road trip," Audrey said with a smirk.

For the first time since her parents died, Victoria grinned broadly. Her eyes narrowing, she savored the wicked glee deep in her chest. It wasn't joy. It was vengeance.

"Yep," she said. "We're going to Santa Barbara."

CHAPTER FIVE

As she left the bank, Victoria held the notebook under one arm and savored the weight of the pouch in her palm. A few of the crystal tips poked her gently through the fabric, the gems shifting a bit with every step. Her mind buzzed, and she walked with her eyes on the ground, totally consumed by her thoughts. The bank's tiled floor quickly became the concrete of a sidewalk outside. The heels of Audrey's sneakers led the way and, after a few minutes, the concrete turned asphalt under her feet as they reached the parking lot. A gentle breeze toyed with her hair, but the pouch was all she could manage to concentrate on besides her overwhelming need to reach Santa Barbara. To find Fyrn Folly. To get answers.

Without warning, a chill ran down her spine.

Not fully understanding why or how, she knew something was wrong. Out of instinct and with no plan or idea of what was happening, Victoria ducked to the ground and pulled Audrey down with her.

A blaze of fire roared over her head and hit the side of a

building, and an alarm went off somewhere nearby, screeching in her ear. A car alarm blared. Not far away, a woman screamed.

Heart thudding, Victoria scanned the parking lot. Cars. A white van. A dozen empty spots. And there—across the way, a familiar man with pointy ears stormed toward them, a nasty grin on his face. He wore a new suit today, one without blood.

Luak.

He lifted one hand, and another swath of fire sailed toward them. On impulse, Victoria lifted her arms to protect herself, and once again the shield appeared before her. It was larger this time, big enough to protect both her and Audrey as the flames rained onto the metal. The handle in her palm began to heat up, searing her like a hot stove, and Victoria cursed under her breath.

"We may never get another chance to kill him," she said, gritting her teeth as she strained to keep the heavy shield in position.

Audrey nodded and pulled the gun out of her backpack. After fumbling with the clip for a moment, she managed to shove it into the base of the handgun and cocked the weapon.

Victoria eyed Audrey. "How the hell did you know what to do?"

Audrey grinned. "You and that woman were taking forever to put back the empty deposit box, so I looked up how to load this kind of gun while I waited for you two. I'm shit at it, though."

"Better than me. Shoot that asshole."

Audrey smile wavered, but only for a second. She

frowned with grim determination and, just as the flames subsided, lifted the gun above the shield. Pausing for only a second, she opened fire. The recoil kicked her backward, and she stumbled.

The sound of gunshots by her ear reminded Victoria of sticking her head in an iron pot as a child and banging on it with a metal spoon. Her ears began to ring almost immediately, and she couldn't even hear herself cursing.

Luak stumbled, and the blaze of fire stopped. Victoria peeked over the shield as he staggered backward, hand on his chest. A hole in his sternum pumped fresh red blood. Falling to his knees, his mouth moved as if he were yelling something, but Victoria couldn't hear anything except the incessant ringing in her ears. She wanted to take this moment, to use it to her advantage, but the ringing seemed to mess with her balance. Her shoulder rammed against a parked car, and the shield disappeared from her grasp. Suddenly lighter, she fell onto her palms.

Audrey screamed, and the gun shook in her hands. Luak grinned, his hand outstretched, and it didn't take much for Victoria to figure out what he was about to do.

"Throw it!" she shouted.

Audrey tossed it into the air. Seconds later, the weapon exploded. Shrapnel shot every which way. Victoria grabbed Audrey and pulled her to the ground, lifting her hands over her head and hoping against hope the shield would appear. The magic in her arm granted her wish, and the heavy weight of the shield pushed against her arms and shoulders. They huddled close, debris smacking the shield with the force of hail.

And, once again, the shield disappeared on its own.

"Christ, I wish I could control that stupid thing," she muttered, glancing around the parking lot. She tried to stand but once more fell, her head reeling from the explosion. Skin still hot from the shield, she was surprised when her knuckles brushed something cold—a metal coil. She blinked herself out of her daze to find the burned remnants of her parents' journal. All that was left was a large "O" on a piece of the cover that had blown several feet away. Although the pouch of crystals had slid under a nearby car, not a single page of the journal had survived.

"You goddamn bastard!" she shouted.

Without thinking, not caring what happened next, Victoria charged him. His gaze shifted from Audrey to her, and he lifted his hand as he had so many times already. But Victoria didn't care about being burned. She cared about stabbing him. Making him bleed. Making him beg for mercy that wouldn't come.

A dagger appeared in her hand, made from the same brass-like metal as her shield. A few clockwork cogs were embedded within the glistening hilt, and the elegant blade curved toward its tip. It was cool to the touch like a river rock, and its appearance derailed her completely.

Shit, this is new.

Her concentration lost, the dagger disappeared, and a hailstorm of fire crashed into her. She sailed back, skin singed by the flames, and landed hard against a parked car. Its alarm went off, adding yet another note to the chaos. She slid to the ground, nursing her arm as the world tilted around her. She tried to stand, but it was as if everything shifted to the left each time she tried. She fell against another car, head throbbing.

Everything that followed was a blur. Someone grabbed her. A car door slammed shut. An engine roared to life, and somewhere in the midst were sirens. Screeching tires. A man's familiar voice cursing loudly. And then, finally, nothing but the soft sound of a pop song playing on the radio.

Victoria could barely think. She wanted so badly to shake off the wounds, to shake off whatever had happened to her. She wanted—

"Holy. Shit." Audrey's voice.

"What? What is it?" Victoria said, slurring.

"Your arms, Victoria! What the hell is happening to your arms?"

Vision starting to clear, Victoria stared down at her arms. They were almost black as soot, burned and charred by the flames. Blisters covered the skin like boils, but she couldn't feel a thing. As she watched, the dark soot began to lighten to her normal skin tone. The blisters faded, smoothing away until her familiar skin covered her arm, not a scar in sight.

As the burns disappeared from her body, the ringing in her ears faded. It was as if her body had reset, returned to normal. Within a few minutes she sat up straight, bones cracking and realigning in her back. One popped into place at the base of her neck, sending a delightful shiver down her spine.

She flipped down the passenger seat visor and studied herself in the mirror. She looked good as new, save for the singed clothes on her otherwise perfectly healthy body.

Gaping, she just stared at Audrey, not altogether under-standing what had just happened. Someone blared their horn, and Audrey corrected the car, arms locked and shoulders tense as she stared out the front windshield and drove through the Seattle suburb.

"We got lucky, Victoria," Audrey said.

"What are you talking about? We lost him."

"We lost—are you kidding me? *I* nearly lost *you*!" Audrey shouted, knuckles white from her grip on the wheel.

Victoria leaned back, surprised at Audrey's tone, and she didn't know what to say.

Tears filled Audrey's eyes. "I thought… When that fire hit you, I thought…I really thought I'd lost my best friend, Victoria. Whatever this thing in you is, we don't understand it. You can't control it. And you cannot go after this guy again until you can."

Victoria frowned. "Don't you dare tell me what I can and can't do!"

"Listen to yourself! You're being an absolute idiot!"

"Hey, we didn't die."

"Victoria!"

Victoria groaned and stared out the window, not wanting to look at Audrey. As houses whizzed by a bit too quickly for a back road, her mind cleared. Guilt slowly piled onto her shoulders, weighing on her heart.

That had truly been reckless.

"I'm sorry, Audrey. I wasn't thinking."

"No, you fucking *weren't*."

Victoria rolled her eyes. "I already said sorry, Ma."

Audrey grumbled nonsensically for a moment before raising her voice loud enough to hear. "We should get the hell out of this city."

"What? But he's here! I just need to practice. I'll get the hang of it. I'll—"

"No! Come on, V. I hadn't seen this guy before, so I didn't know any better. He's deadly. He's a killer, and he wants you. And probably me. He didn't look very happy when I shot him."

Victoria smirked victoriously. "Serves him right."

"Look, V, I don't think we should attack him again until we know more about what's really going on," Audrey said quietly.

Victoria grimaced.

Audrey smacked her palm on the wheel. "I'm serious. We need to get to Fairhaven. We need to find this Folly fellow and figure out what it is your parents discovered. We need information, not an attack plan. Not yet."

Victoria sank into her seat and crossed her arms, staring out the window as she scowled. She couldn't deny how badly their asses had been whupped back there in the parking lot. The more she thought about it and the more she stared at her now-healed hands, the more she had to agree. This was too much to process at once, and Luak had far more experience with magic and this world of Oriceran than either of them. They needed answers and information before they went after him again.

Armed with nothing but her hatred, some crystals, and a weird-ass magical artifact Victoria didn't understand, they would find Fairhaven. Luak's days were numbered...

...as soon as Victoria could figure out how the hell to kill him.

CHAPTER SIX

About four hours after the incident outside the bank, Audrey reclined the passenger seat of her car and set her sock-clad feet on the dash. The warm summer day filtered through the sedan's open windows as they cruised on the southbound I-5 freeway. She was grateful Victoria had been willing to listen to reason. Now, a few hours and a supplies trip later, they had already put fifty miles between them and the psycho killer stalking Victoria.

Hopefully.

Victoria drove, one elbow on the driver-side door as she rested her head against her fist. She stared through the windshield, head bobbing a little bit to the slow and catchy song on the radio. This moment, right here, was the antidote to everything they had experienced thus far. Peace. Quiet. A luxurious moment of calm.

It was great to see her friend happy, if only for a brief window of time.

Audrey glanced through the back window at the empty road behind them as they sped toward Olympia, Washington. Their hometown had long ago disappeared over the horizon. And after the day Audrey had had, good fucking riddance.

Her stomach rumbled. "Hey, you want to stop for Mexican in a bit?"

"And have to deal with you farting for an hour after? No thanks."

"Mean. *So* mean."

Victoria chuckled.

Audrey tapped a drum solo against her door, humming along with the vaguely familiar song on the radio. She recognized the chorus, but that was about it.

Unfortunately, only the letter from Mr. and Mrs. Brie and the bag of crystals had survived Luak's attack. It meant they didn't have the directions to Fairhaven anymore, and that spelled trouble. Thankfully, Victoria had scribbled what little she could remember from her scan of the spiral notebook on the back of the letter. It wasn't much, but it would work.

Hopefully.

Funny, Audrey was usually the jackass, not the optimistic one.

Still humming, Audrey tilted her head ever so slightly to look at a passing sign and caught the vague gray silhouette of someone in her backseat in her peripheral vision. She screamed, turning in her seat to find a man with skin as white as the lines in the road beneath them. He had pointed ears not unlike Luak's, and long blond hair fell like silk threads over his shoulders. He slumped in her backseat, legs spread as he examined his nails.

Audrey, on impulse, grabbed one of the full water

bottles under her feet and threw it at him. He didn't flinch, didn't even move. It sailed straight through him, rebounding off the backseat cushion.

Victoria slammed on the brakes. The car skidded, wheels screeching, drifting a bit as she slowed to a stop on the empty highway. She spun, unbuckling her seatbelt as she put some distance between her and the stranger who had appeared so suddenly in the car with them.

"Who the hell are you?" Victoria cocked her arm as if ready to throw a punch.

Audrey gestured at the strange man in her backseat. "What, you think you can punch him? Did you not see the water bottle sail right through him?"

"Yeah, I missed that. I was busy not driving off the road."

"Can the sarcasm, V. This magic shit is freaking me out!"

"It's not like I—"

"Carry on. Don't mind me," he interrupted.

Audrey hesitated, and Victoria lowered her arm as they both studied him. He took a deep breath and let out a long, slow sigh, never taking his eyes off the windshield.

"Who are you?" Victoria repeated.

"I'm really quite harmless. My name is Shiloh, and I'm connected to that," without looking away from his nails, he pointed toward the blade embedded in her arm.

Victoria frowned, rubbing the dagger with her thumb unconsciously as he spoke. "What do you mean?"

"I go where you go. I see what you see. I'm connected to you, and you to me."

Audrey frowned. "What are you, a freaking ghost poet?"

Victoria shushed her and returned her attention to Shiloh. "You're connected to this thing? What is it?"

"Does it matter? You'll probably die soon, just like all the others."

"Hey!" Audrey shouted.

Shiloh shrugged and looked out the backseat window. "Just my luck, too. Not a big fan of people, and yet I meet so many."

Audrey looked at Victoria, shrugging her shoulders a bit as they did the thing where they could talk without speaking. *What the hell is up with this guy?*

Victoria scoffed and rolled her eyes. *Hell if I know.*

Audrey nodded subtly toward him. *Think he's dangerous?*

Victoria hesitated, eyeing the bored man. She pursed her lips, eyebrows raised. *I have no fucking clue.*

Audrey sighed.

Their moment of panic gone, he did in fact seem fairly harmless. Altogether useless, but harmless. Audrey sank back into her seat, tilting a bit toward the front windshield but never letting Shiloh out of her sight. He continued to sulk, chin almost to his chest as he sat in silence.

Victoria slumped in her seat and tugged her seatbelt back on, shifting the car into drive and slowly accelerating again. They drove in silence with only the music to keep them company, its steady rhythm pumping through the speakers. Every now and then Audrey would look behind her, and she caught Victoria doing the same.

"I don't like this song," Shiloh said, lying down and stretching out across the backseat as though he owned the car. He set his feet by one of the windows, ankles crossed.

For a second, no one did anything. Then, slowly,

Victoria changed the station. A heavy metal song came on, the vocalist screaming as the drummer banged out a solo. Shiloh began to gently bob his head, always out of tempo.

Victoria and Audrey glanced at each other, and Audrey couldn't help herself. She laughed.

One magical artifact fused with her best friend? Check. One psycho serial killer on their tail? Check. One weird-as-hell ghost-elf haunting their car?

Why the fuck not?

CHAPTER SEVEN

Toward the end of the first day of driving, Victoria pulled into a gas station so they could refuel both their car and their stomachs. It was important not to stay long in one place, at least not now.

Audrey hopped out of the car and whipped out a debit card. "I got this, V. Can you find us some food?"

"None for me," Shiloh said in the backseat.

Victoria flinched, and Audrey jumped at the voice. They both stared at the ghost in their backseat, then shared a fleeting glance as Audrey rolled her eyes. "Yeah, I figured, Legolas."

"My name is Shiloh, human girl. Get it right," he said, cheek resting on his fist as he stared into the dark sky.

Victoria shook her head, biting back a grin. "Thanks for handling the gas, Audrey."

As she stepped out of the car, Victoria's skin crawled with discomfort and the vulnerable sensation of being watched. Her eyes scanned the rest stop, taking in every detail she could. Blue sedan parked by the door. Two people in the cabin, plus one kid in the back seat, judging by the small head. The only other car was a beat-up green SUV tucked out of sight in the back corner by the dumpster, probably an employee's based on its location. Inside, only two silhouettes meandered the aisles. No one waited at the cash register.

The hairs on her neck stood on end, and she gritted her teeth harder with every step she took toward the store. Nothing new. Ever since she had seen Shiloh in the back seat and learned that there was a ghost—or whatever—attached to this strange thing shoved all up in her arm, she felt as if someone were standing over her shoulder and watching her every move.

It screwed with her mind, not to mention her nerves.

She entered, a blast of air conditioning hitting her in the face as a bell jingled. Rows of Twinkies, beer, and power drinks led the way toward the blue restroom sign hanging in the back of the store. She needed to wash her face and take care of some of the sweat sticking to her from a day on the road.

As she pushed open the ladies' room door and surveyed the scene, she couldn't help but sigh with relief. Empty. Two stalls. One sink. Red light flashing on an empty paper towel dispenser. The door slammed shut behind her, and she locked it to give herself some privacy. Palms on the filthy counter, she leaned against the sink and stared at her reflection in the foggy mirror.

Same honey-colored skin. Same green eyes. Same pale-pink lips. And yet, she felt like a different person. She examined her arm, still safely hidden by her long-sleeved shirt, and fanned the sweat still clinging to her neck. She gingerly lifted the sleeve to study the relic that had given her these strange powers. The metal tendrils of the dagger's hilt were fused seamlessly with her skin to the point where she almost couldn't tell where one started and the other began. She noticed a few twinkling jewels embedded in the brass, something she hadn't registered before. Rubies, from the look of it. Strangest of all, the hilt had four gaps in it that showed the linoleum floor clear through her arm. No blood. No bone. Nothing. Just open space.

No wonder her dad had always worn long sleeves. This thing freaked her right the hell out.

A stabbing sensation burst through her chest at the thought of her dad, at the thought of him on the living room floor, burning with the house. She gritted her teeth, both enraged and horrified. All at once, she wanted to both hide and kill.

The shield appeared, cutting through the sink and taking her to her knees with its weight. Water spewed into the bathroom from the broken faucet, hitting her square in the face. She blubbered, trying her best to breathe as she fought to wrench the heavy shield from the floor. Instead, she fell hard on her ass, cursing all the while.

Once again, the shield disappeared as quickly as it had come as soon as she lost her focus. She sat in a puddle of water in a gas station bathroom, a stream of water hitting her in the face. Hands guarding her eyes, she crawled toward the water turnoff valve at the base of the sink and twisted the knob. The torrent ebbed, and she spit out water as she heaved for air.

She surveyed the damage. Half an inch of water slowly drained into the dip in the floor by the first toilet stall. Shards of the porcelain sink littered the bathroom, a hefty chunk resting in the far corner. Little black specks of who-knew-what floated in the makeshift lake she had created, and she studied her hands in disgust.

Her cheeks burned with anger. She needed to figure out how to control this thing, how to—

The shield appeared again, cutting through the pipe just below the water turnoff. The water blasted her in a relentless stream all over again. She cussed as loudly as she could, choking again on the water, hands out to shield herself.

Faintly, she heard Shiloh sigh.

The gas handled, Audrey perused the cookie aisle as she waited for Victoria to finish up in the restroom. She faced her toughest dilemma of the day: snickerdoodles or chocolate chip?

The squelching *smack* of wet sneakers on a hard surface caught her attention. She pulled herself away from the cookies just as Victoria, head held high, emerged from the bathroom and headed down the next aisle as if she weren't dripping wet. Her long-sleeved shirt clung to her body, hair sticking to her face like strands of spaghetti as she sucked in a deep breath.

A slow smile spread across Audrey's face before she

could help herself. She gave her friend a once-over, wondering what the hell had happened. But before she could say anything, Victoria stopped in front of the clerk and grabbed one of the pens by the register. She scribbled something and handed him the paper. "Send me the bill."

With that, Victoria passed through the front doors and into the night, the clerk's gaze following her deliberate movements. His jaw slowly dropped, and he snapped his head toward the back bathrooms.

Oops, that was Audrey's cue. Time to go. She tossed the cookies back onto the stand and hurried outside. They could find food somewhere else.

Jogging across the gas station lot, Audrey hopped into the passenger seat as Victoria plopped into the driver's side, still dripping. She stared straight ahead, turning the car on as if nothing were wrong.

"You, uh, want to share with the class?" Audrey grinned.

Victoria hesitated, shivering a little. "I'm fine."

"She broke the sink because she can't control that shield," Shiloh said.

Audrey and Victoria flinched at the same time, both tilting their heads toward the ghost as he once again appeared without warning. In her surprise, it took a second for Audrey to fully process what he had said.

When she did, she burst out laughing.

"Shut up," Victoria said softly, but she chuckled. They caught each other's eyes, their giggling intensifying the longer neither of them spoke. Audrey brushed away the tears in her eyes, core hurting from the laughter.

"Hey, you!" a man shouted, his voice muffled by the closed windows.

Audrey spun in her seat to see the clerk running out of the gas station.

"I already told him I'd pay, and I am *not* in the mood," Victoria said, flooring it. They peeled out of the gas station, Victoria's smile fading as she headed again for the freeway.

"Good thing we brought a change of clothes," Audrey said, shaking her head.

Victoria laughed. "I do feel pretty guilty about this whole thing. There wasn't much left of that bathroom."

Audrey's smile fell. "That bad?"

"This thing, whatever it is, it's powerful. And heavy as fuck." Victoria cleared her throat, shivering again as she continued to drip all over Audrey's car. Truth be told, Audrey didn't even care about the mess. It was perfect, in its own way, because she would never, ever let Victoria forget this had happened.

"I need a shower," Victoria said.

"It's probably for the best. Let's find a place to pull off. And V?"

"Yeah?"

"You need to figure out how to control this thing. What if it happens while we're driving or—"

"Stop! Stop, dude, what the hell? I'm nervous enough as it is." Victoria glared at her.

"You shouldn't drive any more, at least. Once we find a place to pull over, let's switch."

"Fine."

Audrey studied Victoria as the girl stared into the darkening night, the occasional passing freeway lamp illuminating her scowl with soft orange light. They didn't need to discuss this any further. Both already knew the risks. Next time someone might be in that bathroom with her. Whatever Victoria's new powers were, they could destroy things. Hurt people. Maybe even kill.

The two of them needed to find Fairhaven and this Fyrn Folly character—fast.

CHAPTER EIGHT

As the car finally passed into the Santa Barbara city limits, Victoria rolled down the passenger-side window and leaned out to get a better view of the beautiful city. Palm trees lined every street, and the main road ran parallel to the beach. Women and men lay on the sand not far away, basking in the hot California sun. The water glimmered and glistened, the light bouncing off the waves like a million small diamonds.

It was paradise. No wonder there was a magical city hidden here.

Eighteen hours of driving over two days was no mean feat, and after all that time on the road they needed a place to sleep and a hot meal. Still, Victoria couldn't quell her excitement. Soon she would find Fyrn Folly. Soon she would start training to control the magic in her arm. And soon she would have everything she needed to get her revenge.

Her jaw clenched.

Audrey slowed as the speed limit was reduced,

adjusting the towels she sat on to protect her from the sopping-wet seats, still soaked from yesterday. "Okay, Victoria, where am I going?"

Victoria dug into the glove box for the notes she'd scribbled on the back of her dad's letter. A knot caught in her throat as her fingers brushed her father's handwriting, but it wouldn't do any good to dwell on how much she missed her parents. "Looks like we need to find a bridge. The Riviera Bridge. Is your phone charged? I'll look it up."

Audrey handed her the familiar white cell phone with the black skull case, and Victoria typed in her friend's security pin. They'd known each other's access codes for ages.

Her thumb accidentally hit the recent calls button, and Audrey's home phone was on the outgoing calls list. Apparently she had snuck away at some point to check in with her family. Victoria's throat tightened, a bit envious of her friend's surviving family, but she buried the resentment and opened the GPS instead.

"Turn left on West Carrillo Street," a robotic female voice said through the phone's speakers.

"You heard the lady," Victoria said with a grin. She tilted the phone slightly toward Audrey so she could easily glance at the map on the screen while driving. Trees and medians filled with flowers lined the road. Building after building had sparkling white walls and red-tiled roofs, giving the street a classic and uniform look.

"This place is beautiful," Audrey said, leaning forward a bit to stare through the windshield, her eyes lingering on an historic five-story hotel as they passed.

Victoria nodded. "I'm so grateful mom and dad didn't send me to Alaska. Pretty, but cold."

"Would've been easier to hide that thing," Audrey said with a nod toward Victoria's arm.

Victoria's smile fell, and she let out a small huff of air. "I guess that's a good point. It's a little harder to get away with long sleeves in a place where it's never cold."

"Turn right on Olive Street," the robotic female voice interrupted.

Audrey obeyed the little voice coming from her phone and turned onto a side street. Road by road, they obeyed the GPS's directions, twisting and turning as they drove deeper into Santa Barbara's Riviera suburb. So far, not a bridge in sight.

After about half an hour, the GPS led them to the Riviera Bridge. The road led over it, but from what Victoria could remember they had to find a way underneath.

"Over there," Victoria said, pointing to a gravel lot just in front of the bridge. As the car bounced over the uneven path, the thin and winding road led down to a clearing underneath the bridge. The tires crunched over gravel as they inched their way down the steep side-road, Victoria never quite sure whether they would stay on it or fall off and roll down the hill into the reservoir below.

"You have arrived at your destination," the robotic voice said.

The gravel path ended directly under the bridge, which was nothing more than a slender stone arch at most thirty feet over their heads. Concrete walls blocked them in on both sides, and Victoria had a sudden rush of claustrophobia. If Luak found them here, they would be trapped. Dead. He could easily roast them in their car before they escaped, or maybe —

Panicking, afraid the shield would appear at any second thanks to her wild imagination, she threw open the car door and jumped outside. She grimaced, hands over her head as she waited for the inevitable weight on her arm to take her to the ground. Thankfully, it didn't, and she let out a relieved sigh.

Audrey got out as well, throwing the backpack containing the crystals over her shoulder. Looking around, she kicked her door shut. "What next?"

Victoria unfolded the paper and scanned her notes. "We need to touch one of the symbols spray-painted under the bridge. The triangle, I think."

They walked toward the concrete barrier, Victoria on edge as she continued to scan their surroundings. On the other side of the bridge the road ended in forest, gravel fading into dirt and weeds.

Victoria located a couple of strange symbols, their spray-painted lines reminding her of Nordic runes. She reached for the triangle, suddenly doubting how well she had remembered her parents' notes.

"That will electrocute you," Shiloh said from behind her.

She jumped, a little scream escaping her as he once again surprised her. "Christ, will you warn me before you do that?"

"If I remember," he said, shrugging.

So, no, he wouldn't.

She rubbed her temple, annoyed with the ghost elf who had the personality of a thirteen-year-old girl. "So that one will electrocute me if I touch it?"

He nodded.

She waited for him to tell her which one to touch, but he simply stared at his nails.

"Should I touch the square, or—"

"Oh, no, that will melt the skin from your bones."

"Oh, awesome." Victoria rolled her eyes.

Audrey chuckled.

Again, Victoria waited, but the ghost didn't say anything else. She bit her lip to bite back a sarcastic remark and gestured to the symbols on the barrier. "So, which of these will not kill me?"

He huffed. "I think you meant to ask me which will let you inside."

"Oh. My. God," Victoria said, pinching the bridge of her nose in frustration.

Audrey laughed harder.

"Touch that one." Shiloh rolled his eyes and pointed to a crude hourglass-type symbol comprised of two triangles.

"Thank you," Victoria said, gritting her teeth in annoyance as she smacked it with her palm.

Beneath them, the ground trembled. The gravel vibrated from the sheer force of whatever was happening. Pebbles fell off the bridge, and for a fleeting, panicked second Victoria wondered if it would collapse on them.

Gold light shot from the barrier with the symbols, piercing them and sending a ripple of ice down Victoria's spine. A puff of her breath hovered in front of her, suddenly visible despite the hot day. She shivered and watched as the gold energy spread around them like a force field, encapsulating everything within a fifty-foot radius.

The concrete barrier crumbled like a mishandled cookie, the loose chunks of rock disappearing the moment they hit the ground. Bit by bit a jagged hole appeared before them, as tall and wide as a large truck. Stairs appeared one by one, popping out of the ground and leading downward into the darkness. Embedded in both walls, thousands of glowing green crystals lit the way.

"Welcome to Fairhaven. I can take your car," someone said behind them. If a mouse could speak, it would sound like whoever this was.

Victoria spun on her heel and lifted one fist as if preparing to fight, but paused when she saw a little gremlin-like creature with massive winged ears. He—or she—was a murky green color that reminded her of a swamp, with skin covered in little bumps. The creature looked vaguely familiar, and Victoria wondered if she had stumbled across a picture of one in her brief time with their parents' spiral notebook.

She frowned at the memory of the notebook, furious and frustrated that Luak had destroyed such a valuable collection of information. Just one more reason to bash his brains in, she supposed.

"Your car, please," the creature said again, voice squeaky as an old wheel. He lifted the palm of his hand and gestured with his fingers.

"Where are you going to put it?" Audrey scanned the empty gravel lot.

The gremlin creature squeaked in a rapid and unintelligible succession that sounded a bit like laughter. "The car lot, of course."

He snapped his fingers, and the golden light around them shimmered. Through it they could see rows and rows of cars, a few trucks, and even a bus.

Audrey's mouth dropped open, and Victoria was sure hers had, too. Without pausing, Audrey tossed the keys to the creature, who caught them effortlessly. He snapped his fingers yet again, and a golden ticket appeared out of thin air and hovered in front of Audrey. She snatched it, examining the tiny black font on it. Victoria couldn't make out the writing from her angle.

"Enjoy your time in Fairhaven," the creature said with a tiny bow. He snapped his fingers a final time and disappeared into the air. The engine revved to life behind them, only his ears visible over the dash.

Audrey leaned in. "If he wrecks my car—"

"I'll buy you a better one." Victoria grinned.

"Ferrari, you hear me? I want a Ferrari."

"Yeah, right. Not sure I love you *that* much."

Audrey stuck her tongue out and faced the newly formed hole in the wall. "Well, let's do this."

"Don't let anyone see your artifact," Shiloh said, gesturing toward Victoria's arm.

"Why not?"

"They will kill you on sight."

"Jesus," Victoria muttered under her breath. She grabbed her wrist, a little nervous that there was nothing but a thin sleeve between her palm and the artifact she couldn't control.

Audrey put her hands on her hips and stared him down.

"Thanks for the intel, but that would have been better to know much, much sooner."

Shiloh shrugged, arms crossed as he stared into the forest.

Victoria frowned. "What if that valet had seen it, or—"

"He didn't," the ghost interrupted.

"But if he had—"

"He didn't," Shiloh repeated.

Victoria's cheeks burned with annoyance, but she took a breath to cool off. This ghost would be the death of her if she wasn't careful. "We don't need these—people, I guess—in Fairhaven knowing you're a ghost. You should disappear now since the valet can't see us anymore."

"Fine." With that the ghost disappeared into thin air. No *poof,* no warning. He was simply gone.

"Not—" Victoria glanced around, but Audrey's car was rumbling down a row of sedans and kicking up dust so thick she could barely see it.

"God, he's annoying," Audrey grumbled.

Victoria pursed her lips, biting her tongue in the very likely case he could still hear her. To distract herself, she led the way down the stairs. Hand brushing the wall as she descended, she kept her eyes peeled for any change in the shadows. The air cooled with every step. Her mind buzzed as she let her imagination soar at the thought of what Fairhaven might look like. She hadn't realized it would be underground, so perhaps it would be nothing more than a dull network of caves connected by tunnels she would have to learn to navigate. This could be bad. If they needed a quick escape, it would be hard to accomplish with such a long trek to the surface. She wondered how they would find a wizard in a confusing labyrinth below the ground, and how—

Around the next bend, the tunnel ended in a massive cavern that stretched for miles. Birds flew high above, no more than tiny silhouettes. Shimmering green stalactites hung from the cavern's ceiling, bright and brilliant as they glowed with a fire all their own. The one in the center of the cavern reached nearly to the ground to meet a tall white spire ascending from far below, the tallest tower in the city. A white stone palace surrounded the spire, and a network of roads spiraled from the castle like rays from the sun. Crowds bobbed and weaved along the paths far below, thousands of tiny shadows bustling through the massive city. Buildings lined the roads, some of them tilting at impossible angles, some of them swaying slightly.

Beneath their feet, the tunnel became stairs etched into the cliff as it descended to the base of the cavern. It would easily take half an hour to reach the bottom. She gaped as her eyes scanned the underground city.

Audrey whistled. "We're sure as shit not in Kansas anymore."

Victoria nodded, not quite able to form words. This was it—the place where she would find answers, help, and training. Here she would learn everything she needed to know to control the dangerous magic embedded in her body.

She would not rest until she had mastered it *all*.

CHAPTER NINE

At the bottom of the stairs, Victoria couldn't help but pause and stare. Fairhaven was too much to take in all at once.

Despite the glowing green crystals above, nothing had an emerald tint to it. The wide road would have fit four cars across easily, but was instead filled with a bustling crowd of creatures Victoria had never seen before. Some towered a good two feet above her, the ground shaking a bit as they walked, and metal plates not unlike armor covered their shoulders. Some looked like the gremlin who had taken Audrey's car. Most of the crowd were elves like Luak, but they wore elegant gowns and suits. She tensed at their presence, stiffening on instinct, but these elves smiled gracefully. They had class and grace, which Luak lacked.

Everyone who passed stared at her and Audrey, bewildered expressions on more than one of their faces, and she stared right back in wonder.

Her trek into Fairhaven became more intimidating with every step. An unfamiliar underground city. Strange creatures. Only one contact, and she didn't even know what he looked like.

"This might be even harder than I thought," she mumbled.

She walked down the street with no idea of where to go first. Elaborate shops made from black brick lined the road, every window filled with something to sell. From ornate dresses with lace and frills to a massive battle axe coated in blood, there was something for everyone: leather bags, glowing potions, bubbling cauldrons that radiated steam. It seemed as though anything could be bought on this one street alone.

Too bad they had no idea what Fairhaven used as currency.

A little nervous, Victoria pinned her right sleeve hem under the fingers of her right hand, careful to make sure no one could possibly see the artifact in her arm. Every set of eyes seemed to follow them, and no wonder—they were the only humans here.

As they meandered down the busy street, Victoria caught glimpses of life in Fairhaven through the many windows. A little gremlin pointed to a knife in a display and tugged on the shirt of a slightly larger gremlin. In another shop, an elf wearing a tan gown with a black apron over it handed an elaborate leather satchel to a fellow elf whose long blond hair hung in a loose braid over her shoulder. The blonde dropped four crystals into the shop-keeper's palm, and they nodded to each other, muttering words Victoria couldn't hear through the glass.

It clicked for her in that moment: the crystals her parents had left her were the currency here. She shot a fleeting glance toward Audrey's bag, suddenly itching to grab the pouch and keep it close. They hadn't realized what they were before, but now they had to be extremely careful to protect them. It was all they had to survive on, and as strangers to the city, they would need to make every crystal count.

Though most of the shops had nothing set up on the street outside their doors, one store had boxes filled to the brim with what looked like odd, bumpy fruits. The sweet and tangy aromas of mango and pineapple wafted from the boxes, and Victoria's mouth watered. As she studied the display, however, a massive creature emerged from the store, stairs creaking as it descended. The creature reminded Victoria of a bridge troll in a dress. Long black curls framed her round face—at least, Victoria assumed this was a female from her attire. The shopkeeper grinned as Victoria caught her eye, and Victoria returned the smile. Through the window, half a dozen rows of shelves filled the store, each surface lined with trays of meats and casseroles.

The creature said something in a boisterous, high-pitched voice, watching them as she smiled broadly. It was probably another language, but to Victoria, it sounded mostly like humming.

She hesitated. *Crap*. She hadn't even thought of a language barrier as an issue. Desperate and going out on a limb, she cringed a bit and asked, "Do you speak English by any chance?"

"Ah, English. Certainly," the troll-like creature said.

Audrey's eyebrows shot into her hairline. "Wow, I can't believe that worked."

"To succeed in Fairhaven, it helps to know what everyone's saying, even those from above," the shopkeeper said, winking.

Victoria hesitated. Good to know. "Do you get a lot of human visitors?"

The shopkeeper's smile wavered. "No, we don't. Mostly it's the witches and wizards who speak English. I thought you were one of them. You're human?"

Double crap. Victoria had apparently given them away. She would have to be more careful. She tensed, ready to run if necessary. "Is that a problem?"

"Not to me, but don't go bragging about it," the shopkeeper said, winking.

Phew. Victoria relaxed a bit in relief, though Audrey still watched the crowd, many of whom continued to stare.

"My name is Bertha, and I'm happy to serve anyone who enjoys food. You look hungry. Eat!" Bertha gestured to the bins of fruits. Silver peaches filled one of the lower crates Victoria hadn't noticed before, and a half-dozen other types of fruits filled the rest. Now closer to the store, the sweet aroma of the food was tantalizing, almost irresistible.

Audrey nodded, leaning in to whisper. "I'm famished. I think the crystals are currency. You mind using some of them for food?"

"Not at all." Victoria grinned, grateful Audrey had picked up on that too. She knew her friend would always catch anything she missed and confirm the things she didn't.

Bertha gestured to the bins. "What will you have?"

Victoria hesitated, eyeing the shopkeeper. Bertha

seemed kind enough, was certainly happy, and she had been the first person to speak to them so far. Hopefully, she wouldn't take advantage of them and their ignorance of the city. Truth be told, Victoria had no way of knowing even if she did price-gouge them. Unless…

Time for a test.

If a leather briefcase as fine as the one Victoria had seen cost only four crystals, food had to be far cheaper. Time to see how honest Bertha really was.

Victoria reached into Audrey's backpack, careful not to pull the pouch out as she selected six of the smaller crystals. She offered them to the shopkeeper, palm open. "What will this get us?"

Bertha flinched, standing a little straighter as she stared at Victoria's hand. "Little one, that will buy you feast."

Good. This creature was honest. "A feast it is, then."

About one hour and a good meal later, Victoria leaned back in her chair, satisfied and about to burst from all the food. She eyed the leftovers still on the table in the back of the shop, wondering what on Earth she would do with the extra. There was enough left to last them at least two or three more meals—which they would certainly need—but she didn't have any way to preserve it.

"Do you want anything else?" Bertha settled into the chair at the head of the table, her massive frame blocking most of the dark shop behind her. She was an ogre, they had discovered, and more than happy to tell them whatever they wanted to know about Fairhaven and the creatures who lived here.

And they didn't even have to bribe her.

"No, thank you. This was amazing," Victoria said, smiling.

Bertha laughed, a loud and boisterous sound that filled the room and hurt Victoria's ears. "You are too kind, little one. I don't usually get compliments as fine as yours."

Audrey quirked an eyebrow. "Are you kidding? That was some of the best food I've ever eaten in my life."

"No, no, my food is mediocre compared to what you'll find here. Fairhaven is a culinary capital, the kemana with the best food in the world."

"Kemana?" Victoria tilted her head in confusion.

Bertha hesitated and squinted a little, as if surprised by the question. "Are you asking me what a kemana is?"

Victoria nodded, palms a bit sweaty as she tried to get a feel for what she was supposed to know. Even the most innocent of questions was met with complete and utter shock, as though this were all common knowledge.

If only Victoria still had that damn notebook.

Bertha studied her for a moment, almost as if she were trying to decide whether Victoria was playing her for a fool. Finally, she answered. "A kemana is a magical city, one tied to Oriceran, of course. Magic is stronger here thanks to those crystals above us, which store the power and give us the energy we need to thrive here on Earth."

Oriceran—there was that word again. The alternate world where magic lived and breathed like a creature of its own. Apparently, its magic had spilled onto Earth.

"Ah. I figured that's what it was," she lied, forcing a smile.

Audrey shot her a quick glare, the one that meant, *Good going, idiot.*

Victoria squinted her eyes and wrinkled her nose. *Shut up.*

Bertha tilted her head, hiding her mouth as she coughed. "Anyway, no one can beat our food. If you like to sample new tastes, I think you'll enjoy your stay."

"I already am," Audrey said, sighing happily as she sank into her seat.

"Food is one of the reasons I came here. I'm surrounded by my kind." Bertha surveyed Victoria, an odd expression on her face that Victoria couldn't quite figure out. Perhaps it was confusion, or mild curiosity blended with a bit of fear.

Her throat tightened a bit, and she couldn't help wondering if Bertha had somehow figured out what was embedded in her arm. Unconsciously she held her wrist, the solid metal of the dagger under her sleeve still foreign to her touch.

"If you don't mind my asking," Bertha said, leaning in and hunching her shoulders as she lowered her voice, "why are you here?"

Victoria tensed. "What do you mean?"

"You're human."

"You said that wasn't a problem."

Bertha sighed heavily, her thick fingers tapping the table. "Not a problem, but confusing. By law, mankind should never discover us. Those who perform magic outside of a kemana can be put to death for risking the exposure of the magical world. Through the millennia we have found it best if humans don't know we exist. Even the witches and wizards aren't human, although I can't really tell you lot apart. You all look the same to me."

"That's a little racist," Audrey mumbled under her breath.

Bertha continued, apparently not hearing. "Humans don't come to Fairhaven, and on the rare occasions they did in the past, it usually ended in bloodshed."

"Awesome," Audrey muttered again, rolling her eyes.

Victoria leaned toward Bertha. "If humans mean trouble, why did you let us into your shop?"

The ogre smiled, revealing the small white boulders that served as her teeth. "Because I know good from bad. You're strange, ugly little things, but you're good at heart."

"Hey," Audrey muttered at the insult. Victoria grimaced, but she figured it was a matter of perspective. Bertha certainly wouldn't have won any human beauty pageants herself, but she had been kind to them, and Victoria liked her laugh.

Bertha grinned. "You could have tried to cheat me out of my food, or left without paying. But here you are, asking questions and trying to figure out where you fit into our world. My question is why?"

"Fair enough," Victoria said, catching Audrey's eye.

Audrey stiffened, furrowing her brows in concern. *Don't you dare.*

Victoria gently shook her head. *It's fine.*

"We're looking for Fyrn Folly," she said before Audrey could protest.

Bertha laughed, which was not quite the reaction

Victoria had expected. The sound filled the room, almost echoing off the walls. Victoria winced at the sheer volume.

"Why is that funny?" she asked softly, suddenly afraid of the answer.

Bertha wiped a tear from her eye. "You poor, dear things. You came all the way here, descended into our city, and all to find that sad excuse for a wizard? That's a lot of effort put into a mistake."

Fabulous.

"What—"

"He doesn't talk to anyone," Bertha interrupted. "If he walks past someone, he doesn't look them in the eye. He does his errands and he goes home, and that's it. There's talk that he's not what he used to be, or that perhaps he wasn't anything special to begin with. No, if you want help from a wizard, you should see Diesel Armstrong. Diesel is the king's wizard and widely revered. Even though the king doesn't seem to care about his people, he does care about power, and Diesel is the best. But we all love him because Diesel always looks out for those of us who live in Fairhaven."

"Who is he?" Audrey stood and slung her backpack over one shoulder.

Victoria shook her head. "No, we need to go see Fyrn."

"But if Diesel is a better wizard—"

Victoria frowned, glaring at Audrey. Her parents had specifically mentioned Fyrn for a reason. Since merely possessing this artifact could get her killed on sight, she wasn't about to trust anyone her parents hadn't explicitly mentioned.

Audrey lifted her arms in surrender. "Fine, fine. We can at least pay him a visit."

"Where does he live?" Victoria asked Bertha.

Smiling as if they were sweet, stupid little things, Bertha shook her head. "You stubborn human girl! Fine, you can find him on the outskirts of town in the Interval and Highland district."

"Wonderful, thank you. Now, uh, where is that, exactly?" Victoria smiled widely, the grin forced, her cheeks a bit red from how little she knew of the city.

She would have to learn this town inside and out, and fast.

CHAPTER TEN

A rmed with a map and a backpack full of exotic fruit they didn't know anything about, Victoria held the door for Audrey as they returned to the street. Bertha waved from the window, and they returned the gesture.

As they walked down the still-busy street, dozens of eyes followed their every move. It sent shivers down Victoria's spine, but it didn't seem to faze Audrey in the least.

"I like it here," Audrey said, a goofy grin on her face.

"Any attention is good attention, huh?" Victoria said with a smirk.

Audrey laughed.

The road seemed to go on for miles, with intersections every eight to ten buildings as another thoroughfare cut through the main street. A narrow alley separated buildings here and there, each shrouded in shadows.

She checked the map. "I think we need to take a left up here."

"You mean by the sign with the jacket that has four arms on it?"

Victoria quirked an eyebrow and glanced upward. Sure enough, a sign hanging over one of the doors had a traditional suit coat with four arms etched into it.

Fairhaven would take some getting used to.

They continued to follow the map, twisting and turning through roads that got increasingly busier. Quite a few times, hands the size of her face brushed against her back or shoulders. It seemed personal space wasn't really a concept here, and she nervously eyed Audrey's backpack.

"Keep close tabs on the pouch," Victoria whispered.

Audrey nodded, eyes darting over the ocean of heads in front of them. Everyone still watched them, but Victoria was starting to get used to it. On the plus side, it was unlikely any thief would try to steal from them with so many witnesses paying such close attention.

With every step, the towering white palace loomed closer, its spires soaring into the sky. It acted as a sort of backdrop to every street. The beautiful green crystal above the tallest tower glimmered and shone, and the closer they got, the more detail she noticed. The light within the crystal morphed and twisted, reminding Victoria of lava held back by a sheet of frosted glass.

Bit by bit, the busy streets faded away. They began to take narrower and narrower paths, until the two of them could barely walk side by side. It got slightly darker, and the buildings were taller and thinner than the shops they had seen on the main roads. Judging by the laundry hung between the each of the homes, this was Fairhaven's equivalent of the suburbs. Each house had a small patch of land, most of them covered with moss or various vines and walking stones.

Eventually even these dwellings faded away, replaced by larger and larger stretches of moss-covered rock that sat undeveloped. The trail began to wind, cutting a lazy bend into the increasingly steep incline. Above them, nestled into a cliff face that got steadily nearer with every step, was a squat cottage with a roof that reminded Victoria of a wizard's hat. Green smoke puffed out of the cracked chimney. She estimated it would take probably another ten minutes to climb the steep trail that wound its way over the cliff face and ended at the front door.

"Did we take a wrong turn?" Audrey grabbed the map from Victoria's hands, tilting it to the side as she studied it.

"I'm positive we didn't. Look! Is that not the most stereotypical wizard's cottage you've ever seen in your life?" Victoria pointed at it as she paused to catch her breath.

Audrey squinted as if she couldn't see the blatantly obvious cottage, and took a few steps forward. She shuddered, and ripples of gold light radiated away from her as if she had just walked through the surface of a pond.

"Oh!" she shouted, startled.

Confused, Victoria took a few more steps as well. Nothing happened. She didn't shiver, nor did she feel a chill run down her back as she had expected. The cottage remained visible, same as before. "What just happened?"

Audrey pointed up the cliff. "Before all I saw was rock, but as soon as I stepped through…well, whatever the hell that was, I could see the house plain as day. Do you think he has some kind of forcefield around his cottage?"

Victoria laughed. "This isn't Star Trek. He might have cast a protection spell, though. He is a wizard, after all."

Audrey hesitated, peering at Victoria. "But it didn't work on you. You saw the cottage the whole time, right? I didn't."

Victoria nodded, her lips a thin line as she tried to understand what had happened. It must have been the relic in her arm, since nothing else set her apart from Audrey. All the more reason to figure it out. The thing was filled to the brim with powers, and she didn't understand any of them.

They headed up the trail, puffing a bit as they finally reached the top. Without waiting to catch her breath, Victoria knocked on the door.

It opened immediately, as if someone had been standing there waiting for them to knock. Inside the front door stood a tall man wearing a blue cloak and a scowl. He wore a pointy hat with a brim as wide as his shoulders, and he had three braids in his long white beard. He leaned on a five-foot-tall walking stick with a glowing green stone set into the top.

Victoria smiled charmingly. "Hi. You don't know me, but—"

"What the hell are you doing here?" he snapped.

"Hello to you, too," Audrey said.

He snorted, and a bit of gray smoke rolled out of his nose. "You two are human. Humans don't belong in Fairhaven. This is a magical city, filled with magical folk. It doesn't make any sense for you to be here unless you're bringing trouble with you. So, out with it! What the hell are you doing here?"

"The trouble thing," Audrey said, crossing her arms as she leaned against the doorframe.

"What my friend means," Victoria said with a glare toward Audrey, "is that someone is after us. My parents told me to find you. They said you're the only person who can help me."

"I'm not known for my charity," he said, closing the door.

"Michael and Alison Brie sent me!" Victoria shouted seconds before the door clicked shut.

The door paused mid-creak, and she heard a deep sigh from the other side of the threshold. It swung open again, and he was scowling even harder than before, if such a thing were possible. "Those meddling jackasses are your parents?"

Victoria seethed. Anger hit her hot and fierce, taking her over. Her grief was still so raw that she suddenly didn't care if this guy helped them or not. It didn't matter if they lost their only chance to work with him—no one spoke about her family that way.

Her parents had their enemies, sure. It happened to journalists, especially good ones who asked questions people didn't want to answer to get to the truth that so many tried to hide. But no one, not even an all-powerful wizard, would insult the parents who had loved and cherished her with everything they were.

She kicked open the door, and it slammed against the wall. "Those 'meddling jackasses' are dead, killed by some fire-breathing asshole, and I'm going to learn how to kill him if it destroys me. They told me you are the only one I can trust. Why would they say that if you hate them so much?"

His demeanor shifted ever so slightly, and the scowl

disappeared. Now he studied her as if she were an interesting book, and she honestly wasn't sure if that was an improvement or not. He tapped the floor with his cane. "Michael and Alison nearly got me put to death for treason, child. They chased things they didn't understand for the thrill of discovering answers, and it never occurred to them that perhaps the truth was something they didn't really want to know. Worst of all, they tampered with things they didn't understand, a trait they seem to have passed on to you."

Fast as lightning, too quickly for an old man like him, he grabbed her arm and lifted her sleeve to reveal the dagger embedded into her skin. She yanked her hand back too late, hiding the artifact as quickly as she could.

He leaned in, eyes narrowing. "They were an utter nuisance, and as far as I can tell, you're no different. Good day, Miss Brie."

The door slammed in their faces, and all the lights went out at once. The smoke coming from the chimney stopped, the last puff dissolving into the air.

Victoria gaped at the door, baffled by what had just happened. Her one lead, already dry.

"Asshole!" Audrey kicked the door. The knocker bounced once, but no one answered. It was as though he had evaporated into thin air.

Hell, he was a wizard. He probably had.

Overhead, the glowing green crystal slowly dimmed. It reminded Victoria of dusk, and the growing shadows around them reinforced her theory. It seemed that in this underground city where they didn't have the sun, they had found a way to simulate the times of day.

"Please tell me you have a plan," Audrey said, hands on her hips.

Victoria gritted her teeth, eyes wandering over the city below. Given how long it had taken to get here, it would be dark by the time they found an inn—if they found one at all. They had money, sure, but she didn't like the idea of trying to find a place to stay in the middle of the night. Walking through the streets had been scary enough when the roads were busy, and she couldn't imagine trying to find her way around in the dark. They had already attracted a lot of attention, and she wondered what kind they would get when there weren't so many witnesses.

She rubbed her eyes. "Tomorrow we locate an inn. We have to find a place to stay, since Fyrn Folly hasn't exactly been hospitable."

"And tonight? Sleep on his doorstep?"

They needed someplace safe, out of reach, and out of sight. Victoria studied her surroundings, eyes crawling up the wall as she fought to come up with an idea.

High above, she spotted a cave. A steep trail led to it, so steep and irregular it reminded her of stairs. In fact, the longer she looked, the more caves she saw. Some had thin trails snaking to them, but most were nothing but holes in the rock. She pointed to the closest one with a path, probably a five-minute walk away. "There."

The light began to dim faster now, and Victoria headed toward the cave without waiting for Audrey to agree. Audrey followed, grumbling under her breath about sleeping on the ground.

When they reached the cave Victoria peeked in, half-afraid she would find a pair of glowing eyes staring at her.

Thankfully, she was met only with darkness and a shallow, eight-foot deep depression.

She sat down, stretching her legs in the space that was barely big enough for them both. She looked out at the city, and even though she was uncomfortable, she had a brilliant view. The magnificent white castle was front and center, and the roads radiating from it like sunbeams reminded her of the sunny California beach not far away. A few buildings swayed in the growing night, leaving slight streaks in her vision as the final glow faded. Lights shone in some of the windows, the effect not unlike stars in the sky.

Audrey stretched out on her stomach, chin on her hands as she stared across the city. "What have we gotten ourselves into, V?"

Victoria blew a raspberry, tapping one finger on the dusty rock. "An adventure."

Audrey snorted, but a smile spread across her face. "You're a hopeless optimist, you know that?"

Victoria nodded. "You love it."

Audrey offered a fist, smiling. "To the end?"

Victoria fist-bumped her bestie. "To the end."

CHAPTER ELEVEN

Luak strolled through one of the hallways in the magnificent Fairhaven Palace, hands behind his back as he gloated about the fools who had let him in. As he passed, a servant in a crisp blue dress pressed herself against the wall, eyes wide. His grin broadened.

One day this would all be his, and he was so very close.

He was on his way to see King Bornt, ruler of Fairhaven and descendant of a once-fearsome family line. Now the elf could barely string sentences together without his advisors' approval. Luak smirked. It had been almost too easy to infiltrate this place.

Time to convince the king to hand it over.

Even though Luak had lost track of that girl with the artifact he wanted, this was still a good day. True, he had been shot, but an elf didn't rise to his level of power without expecting and preparing for setbacks. He resisted the urge to rub the still-healing bullet wound in his chest, grimacing as pain blistered down his torso. He would make sure to find the girl's friend as well so that he could torture her as punishment for the gunshots.

As he approached the king's council chamber, he could hear the ruler's tinny voice, muffled as it was by the thick wooden door. Always eager to eavesdrop, he leaned against the wood, his keen ears picking up what most others would not.

"...but that creature is advancing up the lower levels of the city," the king said.

"We have no evidence of that," a woman replied. Her voice shook, betraying nerves. Luak tried to put a name to the voice, but he didn't quite recognize her. He suspected this was the Speaker of the Senate, whom he had heard of but not yet met.

Someone banged their fist against a wooden surface, likely the table. "It killed three sewer workers last night. We've blamed a wayward thief, but we can't keep that up. If the public finds out what's really going on, they will panic."

Hmm. Luak had heard enough. He opened the double doors with a flourish, the thunder of the wooden panel banging against the wall enough to startle birds off the balcony railing. The voices stopped. Light streamed through a skylight, revealing the famed White Tower as it stretched toward the crystals above.

"The public will do more than panic, my good king," Luak said, allowing only the thinnest of smiles. Arrogance and confidence, when blended together, could intimidate the king like nothing else.

King Bornt stood taller, as did the three people surrounding him. Luak recognized the goblin Minister of Finance, Grange, as well as General Force, the king's

second-in-command and leader of his army. But an unfamiliar woman also stood beside the king, draped in a white
robe with a gold hem, her long black hair pinned into a
bun. A witch, by the lack of point to her ears. This must be
the speaker of the Senate, Lady Spry.

"This is a private meeting, Luak," the king said. But the
man's knees trembled, and he balled his hand into a fist.

Nerves. Almost too easy to spot.

It never changed with this elf—he was such a coward.
A disgrace to elves everywhere, honestly. Luak had barely
needed to exert any effort to weasel his way into the
castle, and it would take only a few strategic deaths to
overthrow the king, who had never fought a day in his life.
This man didn't understand strategy, and he didn't even
notice the slow but steady coup taking place under his
nose.

"And I do apologize," Luak said with an insincere bow.
"My keen ears couldn't help but overhear your conversation, and I must warn you—I know your subjects, and they
won't simply panic when they discover the creature
beneath the city."

Lady Spry's eyes widened. "What do you know of the
monster?"

"Only what I overheard a moment ago," he lied.

"And?" She quirked an eyebrow, scanning his face with
her purple eyes.

Luak set a finger on his lips as he flashed a charming
smile. "Your secret is safe with me, I assure you. I
mentioned the monster only so that I could fairly warn our
dear king that his people will revolt if they feel their
government cannot protect them. You *are* taking the

required measures to remove whatever it is that plagues the people?"

"Of course." The king's eye twitched.

A lie.

Luak suppressed his laughter and made yet another insincere bow. The king was ignoring the issue in the hope that it would resolve itself. Luak could see the elf's resolve weakening even faster than he had anticipated.

Beautiful.

Luak would have the city sooner than he expected, which would impress his master to no end. Fairhaven was an important chess piece in a far larger game, and important in ways not even the king fully knew.

CHAPTER TWELVE

Victoria woke to the first rays of the glowing crystal overhead as day slowly spread across Fairhaven. She squinted at the city below, shielding her eyes with her arm as they adjusted to the underground version of daylight. Light glinted off the metal in her arm, and her body tensed as she studied it.

This thing was the source of so much stress, so much trouble. It was the reason they couldn't find another mentor, and yet it gave her powers. It set her apart. Her father had entrusted it to her, and she would never dream of letting him down.

Beside her, Audrey stirred. Her lifelong friend rubbed her eyes, groaning as the crystals' light danced across her face. "Ugh, what time is it?"

Victoria laughed. "No idea. Think they use our method of telling time? It's probably blorg o'clock or something."

Audrey chuckled, rubbing her back. "Let's find somewhere else to sleep tonight, deal?"

"No kidding." Victoria cracked her back, fingertips brushing the roof of the small cave as she stretched.

They stared at the city for a moment, Victoria taking it in as she debated her options. They had no allies, no direction, and no clue how this culture operated. They did have a handful of crystals, but she wasn't even sure what they were worth here.

Basically, Victoria had nothing.

The good news: her dad had often called this kind of situation Ground Zero, and Ground Zero had never fazed him.

The only way out is up, he would say. *When you start at the bottom, pretty much any move is a good one.*

Jaw tensing, she lifted her chin in defiance. She could handle this.

Victoria needed a mentor, plain and simple. Somewhere in the city, there was a person she could trust, someone who understood what was in her arm and how to control it. Even though they had banked on that person being Fyrn, this was a vast city filled with magical creatures and people who understood the power she now possessed.

It was of utmost importance that she find an ally. She needed someone to teach her how to control her new gifts.

Her back ached, a rippling pain going down her spine, and she debated for a moment about what was most important. Maybe they needed a place to sleep now, and the mentor could come second.

That was it: a steady source of food and a bed, then a mentor.

Easy-peasy.

She leaned against the entrance to the cave, crossing her arms as her mind wandered and her eyes slipped out of focus. Bertha had mentioned another great wizard, Diesel something. Though Shiloh had warned her that she couldn't trust anyone since her magic dagger-thing made her into someone worth killing, perhaps Diesel would be more open to discussion than Fyrn had been. Maybe he would be willing to help her.

It was a life-or-death risk, one she didn't like taking. She wouldn't choose right this moment. Before she trusted Diesel with her life, she wanted to meet him and see what he was like. In the meantime, she needed to practice and stay out of public as much as possible. She had already destroyed a bathroom sink, but her abilities would have greater consequences here. If someone saw her accidentally summon the sword or shield, it could get her killed on the spot.

It could get both her and *Audrey* killed.

She glanced over at her friend, who stretched her legs on the hard rock floor as she stared at the distant palace. Her eyes scanned something, likely getting a feel for where they were. Audrey had a gift for directions, remembering how to get to a place after only being there once. It was an ability Victoria truly did not understand, but one she was grateful to have on her side.

But she couldn't ask Audrey to live this life with her—it just wasn't fair. Audrey had a knack for entrepreneurship. Victoria already knew that someday, Audrey would be worth millions and own several nationwide chains or online businesses or something. She had several applications out to the nation's top entrepreneurship programs, and Victoria couldn't steal her away from that life.

"Audrey," Victoria said, hesitating as she tried to figure out how to word this, "you don't have to stay. You didn't bargain for any of this. I would understand if—"

"I'm going to stop you there," Audrey said, cutting off the speech with a wave of her hand.

Victoria scoffed and gestured at the city. "But look at this. We have no home, no mentor, no clue what the hell this thing in my arm is. Up there, you have a life. A family. A future. College. Ambition. What do you have here?"

Audrey's smile faded. She grabbed Victoria's shoulders and held them until her bestie made eye contact. "I have you."

Victoria couldn't help herself—she grinned. "I thought I was the gooey, optimistic one. When did you get all sentimental?"

"Shut up. Ass." Audrey laughed and let go, using her palms to stretch her neck.

"But your parents—" Victoria's eyes slipped out of focus, and the flickering joy she'd enjoyed since she came to Fairhaven disappeared.

"They'll be fine."

"I know, but they'll worry if you don't check in." Victoria tugged her cell phone out of her pocket, which had zero bars and a dying battery.

"Hey, listen. Mine's not dead yet, so I'll switch it off to save battery. I'll check in next time we hit the surface. They know I'm taking care of you, and I'll tell them I'm going to travel the world with my rich, sad friend."

Victoria laughed. "Just don't tell them the full story."

"No way. And hey, it's not a huge lie." Audrey gestured to the vast city below.

Victoria put her hands on her waist. "This won't be easy. Do you trust me?"

"To the bitter, gruesome end."

Victoria rolled her eyes. "It doesn't have to be *bitter*."

Victoria would need to buy them cloaks or something. They got way too much attention in their dirty jeans and tee shirts.

They walked through the streets to Bertha's, where they knew they could at least get some food from someone they could trust not to rip them off. Once again, hundreds of eyes watched her every step. It was worse today, far worse. Everywhere she looked, someone was already looking at her. The sensation of eyes on the back of her neck made the hair on her body stand on end.

She fucking hated it.

Taking a moment to pause and catch her breath, Victoria peeked in the window of a nearby shop filled to the brim with dresses. Gold, red, and green fabric lined the walls, and a mannequin in the window display modeled an ornate gown fit for a queen's coronation.

In the glass, Victoria caught her and Audrey's reflections. With tousled hair and smudged day-old makeup, they looked like shit.

"We look like we're doing the walk of shame," she said with a chuckle.

Audrey snickered and gestured for Victoria to follow. "Come on, let's get going. I need some food."

When they finally reached Bertha's, she already stood outside with the crate of lumpy pink fruit in her hands. As they neared, the aroma of mangoes filled Victoria's nose. Her stomach growled on cue.

Bertha smiled broadly as they approached and set the box on the dusty cobblestones. "How are my favorite customers?"

"Hungry!" Audrey said.

Victoria smiled warmly, surprised by how happy she was to see the ogre who just yesterday had called them ugly. "How's your morning, Bertha?"

"Same as ever, I suppose," she said with a smile and a sigh. "I love being here, but I certainly wish I could keep my crates outside without them getting stolen. They're cumbersome to carry."

"Oh, well, we can help you with that," Victoria said.

Audrey nodded. "What do you need done?"

"Oh, I couldn't trouble you—"

"Nonsense. Order us around," Victoria said with a grin.

Bertha laughed and gestured through the door toward several barrels and crates underneath the front window. "Very well, little ones. Here's what needs to go out."

Victoria and Audrey carried the crates out one at a time, grunting a little with effort as they helped her set up the outside display.

"Yikes, these are heavy," Victoria mumbled.

Audrey chuckled, but didn't reply. "What's for breakfast, Bertha?"

The ogre nodded at a crate filled with what looked like

orange bananas. "These are some of my favorites. I have a few candied in the fridge, and I'll let you taste them. I like to put them on snarx eggs."

"Snarx eggs! I love those." Victoria laughed, unable to bite back her sarcasm. This place was almost too much to take in.

Audrey rolled her eyes. "Smartass. Bertha, what the hell is a snarx?"

"Nasty creatures, snarxes. They look like basilisks or giant snakes, but they have a hundred stubby little legs like a centipede. Though the eggs are only the size of my head, a baby is ten times your size once it hatches, little one."

Victoria shuddered. "Yikes. Do any live here?"

"Haven't heard of one in a decade, but don't go into the lower tunnels. You never know what you'll find in the Fairhaven sewers."

Noted.

Audrey lifted the last crate. "They're huge, huh? What do they eat? Moss and stuff?"

"Trolls and pixies, mostly. They love little critters."

"Trolls are little?" Victoria quirked an eyebrow.

"About five inches tall, yes. Annoying little pests. But you watch out for those snarxes, do you hear me? Steer clear. One of those will gobble you right up if you stumble across it. Teeth like daggers."

"Ick," Victoria and Audrey said together, shuddering in unison.

"That's the last of the crates," Bertha said, clapping her hands. She waved to a lumbering creature as he came out of the store next door. His round face and protruding snout reminded Victoria of a pig. He was one of the tall, armored-plated and barrel-chested beings Victoria had seen yesterday, though admittedly a bit fatter than those she had seen wearing armor. He wore nothing but a stained white apron and the blue skin he had presumably been born with. Thankfully the apron covered anything Victoria didn't want to see, until he bent over and picked up a box by his shop door, exposing his bare ass to all the world. Victoria cringed, looking away.

"Rory, watch my stall, will you?" Bertha asked.

Rory grunted, lifting his hand in a lazy wave.

Bertha led the way inside, toward the kitchen in the back. "The least I can do is make you breakfast. Is that all you needed?"

"That and your charming company," Audrey said with a wink.

Bertha chuckled, a deep rumble that filled the shop. "I think you'll like these eggs. For something so vicious, they taste great."

Victoria collapsed into a chair at the now-familiar table, a plate filled with bread rolls in the middle. She wriggled in her chair as she got comfortable, her back still aching from last night. "We could also use a place to stay. Do you know of any good inns?"

Bertha did a double take, eyes roaming Victoria. "Where did you sleep last night?"

"One of the caves in the cliff face."

Bertha smacked her fist against the counter and shouted something in a language Victoria didn't understand, but she knew the tone full well—cursing. The great, big ogre slapped both palms flat on the table and stared at

Victoria, brows furrowed in anger. "Are you trying to get killed?"

"What? Why, are the caves bad?"

"Bad? *Bad*? Child, do you know what lives in there?"

"Take a wild guess, Bertha." Audrey grabbed a roll from the center of the table and shoved it in her mouth.

"Bandits! Thieves! The pickpockets who steal in our streets! Not to mention the nasty beasts that prefer the deeper caves. Never go in those again, do you hear me?"

Victoria quirked an eyebrow, mind racing. If few ventured there, maybe they could find a cave with no thieves or bandits in it so she could practice controlling her new magic. After all, she would need isolation to learn to wield the thing in her arm.

Bertha yanked open a silver cabinet, and a huff of cold air leaked into the room. She plucked a bowl from within and viciously stirred it with a spoon from the counter. "You humans, honestly! So reckless."

"Where can we stay? We have a bit of cash, so we can pay," Audrey said.

"Cash?" Bertha looked over her bumpy shoulder.

"Money," Victoria said.

Bertha stared at her blankly.

Victoria reached for Audrey's pack, pulling out a few of the crystals from the drawstring pouch her parents left her. She spread her palm, showing Bertha. "These."

"Ah, denni. Our currency is called 'denni.' And never you mind, girls. If you help me out in the mornings, I'll make up my spare room for you. It'll keep you out of those caves." She clicked her tongue, shaking her giant head.

"Oh, Bertha, thank you!" Victoria smiled and wrapped

her arms around the ogre's waist. They didn't fit all the way around.

The shopkeeper patted Victoria on the head. "Of course. I'll have a friend of mine make you some clothes as well. Those human rags won't suit you here. Now, eat up. You two are pitifully thin. I can't do much to fix your strange little faces, but I can at least fill out those figures."

A few hours later Victoria carried a basket of apples out back, wearing a fresh outfit that reminded her of steampunk cosplay. Between the boots and the corset over her white blouse, she loved it. At least Fairhaven had decent fashion. She carried a basket of apples on her hip and rifled through them in search of a ripe one. She couldn't always recognize the strange and magnificent fruits, vegetables, and meats that Bertha prepared, but at least these were familiar. They were also, unfortunately, unfit for consumption according to Bertha. These were set aside as feed for the local farm animals, but Victoria snuck a bite anyway.

As the sweet juice of the bright red apple filled her mouth, she surveyed Bertha's yard. There wasn't much to it: a large shed with a lock on it, a small space paved with bricks, and a wooden fence that blocked most of the view beyond. She could only see the roofs on the second or third stories of the nearby houses, and of course the crystals glowing far overhead.

She still expected to wake up at any moment, to shake herself and realize that none of this could be happening. And yet, with every passing second she fell more in love with the crazy city filled with people who kept calling her ugly.

Something hissed. Body tensing, eyes darting over the yard, Victoria tried to find the source. In the corner, a strange cat-like creature with pink fur and two sets of ears pawed at the dirt. Its fluffy tail curved like a snake, drifting back and forth. Victoria set her basket down and peeked over the cat's shoulder, only to find a small person with wings waving his hands and squeaking unintelligibly.

The cat lifted its paw to strike, but Victoria smacked it on the butt. It screeched, jumping in the air and spinning to face her. It hissed, forked tongue darting through its razor-sharp teeth and hackles raised as it tensed to attack. She yelped in surprise at the hideous-looking creature. It pounced. Surprised, she lifted her hands to catch it, but a shield appeared instead. The cat landed hard against the metal with a loud clang that echoed around them. The shield disappeared as quickly as it had come, and the cat-like monstrosity stumbled across the yard, eyes crossed. After a few seconds of stumbling, it shook its head and ran off, shooting her a nasty glare before it jumped over the fence.

Victoria scanned the nearby houses, but no one watched her. She had gotten lucky, but her luck might not hold. She would need to be more careful.

The little creature the cat had attacked whimpered. Victoria knelt, stretching her hand toward the little guy who cowered on the dusty brick, his back pressed against the wooden fence. He wore a brown tunic with a tiny rope drawstring, thin metal cogs fused with his delicate wings. He watched her through gaps in his fingers, trembling.

"It's okay, you tiny thing," she said softly.

He stopped trembling and stood a little straighter, hands pressed against the wooden fence for support as he examined her. His gossamer wings reminded Victoria of the fairies and pixies in the stories her mother used to read to her when she was a child. But this little pixie had clockwork pieces that clicked in a circle embedded in his shoulder, and another in the middle of his chest. One of his arms ended in a metal claw. He flitted upward, his wings humming as they beat the air, and he flew close to her face. He squeaked, his voice high-pitched and unintelligible, and hugged her nose.

She laughed and stood, happy to have saved the little guy. As she returned to the house she felt something tickle her arm and looked down to find him holding on, his arms and legs wrapped as far as he could around her wrist. She chuckled and lifted him off her, setting him on the ground. "You'll be fine. Just don't play with any more cats, okay?"

Pleased with her good deed, she walked inside as Audrey finished setting some sweet potatoes into another of the baskets. Wiping sweat from her brow, Audrey squinted at Victoria's head. "What's in your hair?"

"Huh?" Victoria reached into her hair to find the little guy holding onto her ear. She chuckled.

"What is that? He looks like a tiny human."

"No idea. I saved him from a cat-thing."

Audrey laughed. "Not even the cats are normal here. At least we have apples and sweet potatoes to remember home."

"You just wait. I bet those potatoes sing when you cook them or something."

Audrey snorted and pointed to the creature in Victoria's hair. "You found yourself a pet already?"

"Guess so. He won't leave me alone."

The floor creaked under the heavy weight of familiar, stomping footsteps. Bertha ducked under the doorframe into the kitchen and clicked her tongue. "Oh, those pixies!"

"He's a pixie?" Victoria asked.

"Annoying things. They were some wood elf's experiment gone wrong, and they escaped about three years ago. They've been bothering us ever since. Never fear, little one, I'll kill him for you. Hold still." Bertha raised her arm, tongue sticking out a bit as she took aim at Victoria's head.

Victoria lunged backward, out of reach, "I'm good! All good, thanks."

"Nonsense. Hold still." This time Bertha grabbed a broom from against the wall. Victoria tensed and shuffled around the table, doing her best to keep it between her and the ogre trying to swat her.

Audrey doubled over with laughter, holding her sides.

"A lot of help you are," Victoria said under her breath as she passed.

Audrey laughed harder, tears in her eyes now.

"Fine, fine," Bertha said, dropping the broom. "Stubborn humans! Keep the stupid thing."

"My own pixie, huh?" Victoria set the little guy in her palm. "I should name you Styx."

Audrey shook her head. "A pixie named Styx. How original."

"Shut up. It's funny."

"If you say so."

Victoria picked up the second basket of apples she

needed to take outside, grinning in triumph as Bertha returned to the front of the shop. So far, she had found two of her three necessities: food and shelter.

Now to find a mentor.

She studied her right hand, the cold metal of the relic in her arm a constant reminder of the unfamiliar tech that had permanently fused with her. She'd defeated a cat with it, but that was hardly a victory. This thing would get her killed if she didn't act fast. With Fyrn out of the picture, she needed to find this wizard named Diesel and hope beyond hope he didn't kill her on sight.

She grimaced, butterflies in her stomach at the thought. Maybe she should practice a bit first, get the hang of summoning at least the knife so she could bluff her way out of a bad situation if everything went south.

Ugh. Weak. She hated it when plans required bluffing, as it left too much to chance. Yet, as she stared up at the glowing green ceiling, the nerves ebbed somewhat. She had found Fairhaven. She had found Fyrn Folly. Her parents had set her on the right path, and she would not fail them. She wouldn't be able to live with herself if she did. Failure wasn't an option.

She nodded to herself, resolute about what had to come next. As much as it would hurt, it was time to train. Hard.

CHAPTER THIRTEEN

Around lunchtime, Victoria ducked through the crowds on Fairhaven's Main Street with Audrey in tow. Bertha only needed their help in the mornings and evenings, and since they had the afternoon off, Victoria figured she should find a place to practice. Styx had nestled in her hair and fallen asleep in her loose curls, so she took him along for the ride.

As she walked through the crowds, she eyed the cliff faces surrounding Fairhaven. Wherever she looked, she found a new cave. There must have been hundreds, thousands even.

It would be the perfect place to practice. The trick would be finding an empty one. That was why Audrey had tagged along. Though neither were exceptional fighters despite their time in kickboxing classes, Audrey threw a mean left hook.

First, though, they needed to get out of town. It wouldn't do for half the city to see them scaling the cliff to a cave. Talk about suspicious. No, they needed someplace on the edge of town, like Fyrn's house.

An idea dawned on her, and she grinned mischievously. His protection spell had hidden everything—his house, the caves in the cliffs, all of it. If they were going to practice, they might as well be hidden completely.

Perhaps the old fart would be useful after all.

Audrey led the way through the streets, most of the route still foreign to Victoria until they rounded a corner and saw the familiar trail toward the old cottage. Victoria's heart leapt in her chest as she scanned the windows looking for signs of life. No lights. No smoke in the chimney.

Bingo.

Styx fluttered by, zipping around their heads as they hurried through the force field while Victoria scanned the cliff. There were at least two dozen caves to choose from, four of which had paths, or at least rocks they could hop across, to the entrances.

From here, she couldn't tell how deep they were. She pointed to the nearest one. "That's the one we slept in last night, right?"

Audrey cracked her back. "Yeah, unfortunately."

"What about that one?" Victoria pointed to the only other one with a real path to it. The others would require a lot of hopping and prayer to reach.

"Let's try it."

They climbed the path, Victoria careful to press her

back against the wall in the narrow parts as she inched along the rock. She peered over the edge—a good thirty-foot drop—and was grateful heights didn't make her weak in the knees. Audrey, however, looked like she was having a rough time of it.

"You're doing gr—"

"No talking," Audrey said, back flat against the wall and eyes wide as she crept along the path.

Victoria suppressed a chuckle and nodded.

Once at the entrance, she leaned toward the cave and peeked in. Darkness. It was deep, and the light only illuminated the first fifty feet. After that, nothing but shadow.

She tensed her jaw, straining her ears to listen. No footsteps. No conversation. No bones or leftover carcasses that would normally litter a creature's den. She held her breath but couldn't hear a thing in the silent cave. No rugged breathing from some other creature, thank goodness. She scanned the cave for signs of life like the remnants of a fire or leftover food, but found nothing.

Carefully, she tiptoed inside. Audrey followed, fists balled and no doubt ready for a fight. Victoria craned her neck as her eyes adjusted to the growing darkness, but she didn't see any moving figures.

"Sweet," she said under her breath.

Audrey yelped, spinning toward Victoria. "*Fuck*, you scared me!"

Victoria laughed. "I think coming all the way out here was a good idea. Fyrn's spell must keep out the creatures and thieves."

"For now."

"Thanks, Debbie Downer."

"I'm just saying we should be careful. You never know when someone—or something—may show up. Besides, Fyrn made it pretty clear he doesn't want us here."

"Noted. What are you going to do while I practice?"

"Keep watch. These caves make me nervous."

"We're fine," Victoria said with a grin.

"Do *you* want to get eaten by a giant centipede? Because I sure don't."

"What, a snarx? Sorry, but it's hard to take something seriously when it sounds like it came out of a Dr. Seuss book."

Audrey blew a raspberry. "Just focus. Go train. I'll be by the entrance."

"Stay out of sight."

"Yes, Ma," Audrey huffed.

Victoria rolled her eyes and stepped into the low light at the back of the cave, careful to stay as far from the entrance as she could. Even this far out of town and protected by a spell, she didn't want anyone to witness her magic.

"Hey, actually..." Victoria set one hand on her hip, tapping her chin with her finger.

Audrey glared over her shoulder. "What?"

"You should spar with me. That might help."

"Hell, no."

"Hey, be helpful!"

Audrey shook her head. "Your shield-thing might randomly appear and kill me. You master solo first, and maybe we'll level up to sparring when I'm sure I won't die."

"Thanks for the vote of confidence."

Audrey blew a sarcastic kiss.

"Ugh, fine." Frowning, Victoria rolled up her sleeves and studied the relic fused to her arm. It glimmered in the low light, the silver and copper metals twinkling like the sea. Styx hovered nearby, cooing as he stared at the glittering metal.

Nothing happened.

Hmm. "Appear."

A glint of light from the metal embedded in her arm blinded her for a second, but that was it.

Pacing, she stared at the magical artifact and wracked her brain to remember what had been different about the times the shield had appeared for her.

Ah, right—moments of fear.

She eyed the cave entrance nervously, but this wasn't quite the same. It wasn't true fear, just unease. She'd felt fear when she thought of Luak, of the way he had charged her—

The shield appeared in her hand, weighing her down like a hundred-pound barbell. She groaned, bending with it as it crashed into the ground and embedded itself in the rock. Styx squeaked with fear and flitted toward the ceiling.

"Damn it," she muttered. She wrestled with the massive shield, trying and failing to dislodge it. Cursing under her breath, she focused her attention on the shield. The memory of Luak faded, and the shield went with it.

She fell to her knees, pain shooting down her legs from the fall. She grimaced, frustrated, annoyance burning her up from inside.

"Calm down," she said softly to herself. With a deep

breath and closed eyes, Victoria slowly cleared her head. She could handle this. She could do this.

It seemed as though her new magic responded to either memories or emotion. At least she had finally narrowed it down a bit.

Success!

Technically.

Sort of.

She braced herself and lifted her right arm, tensing her shoulders as she prepared to summon the shield again. In the parking lot by the bank, the shield had changed size to accommodate both her and Audrey, which meant this thing could morph. Perhaps she needed to try a smaller one, one she could hold. Maybe she could—

A flash of green light from the entrance of the cave blinded her. Only streaks filled her vision. Victoria lifted her arm to shield her eyes, but she still couldn't see.

"What are you doing?!" someone asked, his voice harsh and deep.

Victoria panicked. A massive shield appeared, blocking her entire view of the cave. She cursed, the weight of the massive thing pulling her onto her stomach as it tipped over. The shield disappeared as she fell, and she hit the ground hard.

Covered in dust and gravel, she looked up to see Fyrn's silhouette. Audrey had been frozen in place, one hand reaching for Victoria and mouth open as if she were trying to say something.

"What did you do to her?" Victoria demanded. She pushed herself to her feet, clenching her hands into fists.

He quirked an eyebrow. "You're going to fight me? Really?"

"I don't care if you're a wizard. No one hurts my friends!"

"She's fine," he said, rolling his eyes. "You, however, are an idiot. Why are you still here?"

"We needed a place to practice. We only stayed last night—"

"Not the cave. Here! Fairhaven! You're going to get yourself and everyone around you killed."

"Why? Because I have this thing in my arm?" She lifted her right arm, pointing to the artifact with her other hand to emphasize her point.

He grabbed her hand and lowered it, never touching the relic in her arm. "Exactly. Go home."

"I don't have a home," she snapped.

He groaned, leaning on his staff as he studied her. "And you're here for vengeance."

"That, and I'd like to learn how to control this damn thing."

"You won't."

Victoria gritted her teeth. "Don't tell me what I can and can't do. I'm going to figure it out even if I have to do it alone."

"Right, and how's that working for you?"

"Fine, until you interrupted. If you're just going to waste my time, leave."

Fyrn pointed one long finger at Victoria, voice lowering to a dangerous growl. "Listen here, you—"

Styx flitted behind the old wizard, hands on his tiny

hips as he mimicked Fyrn's motions. He squeaked and mumbled, mimicking Fyrn's voice as well.

"Infuriating pixies." Fyrn waved the creature away, the blow thankfully too slow to hit Styx. Scowling just as he had the first time she met him, the wizard tapped his staff against the rocky floor. "Need I remind you that you're on my property, girl?"

She rolled her eyes. "Fine, I'll find somewhere else. I don't need you."

"Yes, you do. You need someone to teach you about that artifact, but no one here will do it. I certainly won't. If you want to live longer than a week, you will leave this city and never come back."

"Why, because my parents asked you a few questions? You think being an ass is going to make you feel better about it?"

"A little bit, yes."

"Look, they're dead, okay? Dead. Luak killed them, and I'm going to destroy him if it's the last thing I do."

"It will be."

She lifted her hands impulsively, desperately wishing she could strangle this asshole, but refrained from wasting the effort. "I'm going to get justice. If you're not going to be useful, will you at least get the hell out?"

He laughed derisively. "Justice or revenge?"

"Why not both? I doubt my family was the first one on his hit list."

"Do you even know what that thing in your arm is?"

"Take three guesses."

"It's a Rhazdon Artifact. It's feeding off you like a parasite, and as its host you have certain abilities—abilities the people in Fairhaven fear. You will be killed on the spot if anyone so much as sees it."

Victoria studied the metal dagger, buzzing with exhilaration because the old man had finally said something useful. Now she knew what it was called. "You said it's *an* artifact. That means there's more than this one?"

"Many. There are said to be two hundred and three."

"Do they all have the same powers?"

He frowned. "Why do you ask?"

"Maybe there's someone out there who has one and can teach me, since you're being a jackass about all this."

"Insult the only person with answers, sure. Very smart."

She shrugged. She wasn't wrong.

"Anyone with a Rhazdon Artifact would sooner kill you for it than train you to use it. These are items made from dark magic. They're dangerous, and so is anyone who wields one. You should leave. Go back to the human world where you belong. Forget about this thing in your arm and wear long sleeves for the rest of your life. It's for your own good, girl. There's more going on here than meets the eye, and you're going to get everyone who talks to you thrown in jail as a host sympathizer."

"'Host sympathizer?' What are you talking about?"

"It's not just the hosts who are killed on sight. Your friend back there," he nodded toward the still-frozen Audrey, "and the shopkeeper who's feeding you are in danger too."

"How do you know about—"

"Both of them are at risk," he said, ignoring her question. "Both of them can be jailed, tortured, or killed. It's not just the artifact in your arm that's illegal, child. Down here, the belief is that you shouldn't exist. The moment you make a mistake, the moment you summon that magic in public, you and anyone who tries to protect you will be murdered."

She stood a little straighter, back arched and body frozen by the thought. For a moment she couldn't breathe. Seconds passed, and when she regained her composure, she gestured toward the exit. "If you don't mind, I have some horrifying magic to master and a bad guy to kill."

"Fine, get yourself stabbed in the streets," he muttered, limping toward the entrance. He leaned heavily on his staff and snapped his fingers. With the one motion, he both disappeared and released Audrey. She gasped, falling to the ground as she regained movement.

"Fuck that guy!" she shouted, looking over her shoulder.

"He's a bit of an ass, isn't he?" Shiloh asked, suddenly appearing beside Victoria. She cursed, jumping a solid foot to the left as he spooked her.

"Couldn't agree more," she muttered.

Shiloh nodded. "I like him."

Victoria gritted her teeth, rubbing her temples to calm herself. "Of course you do."

CHAPTER FOURTEEN

A few hours later, at Bertha's once more, Victoria leaned against a crate filled with strange purple tomato-ish fruits and stared into the distance. Her training efforts had been pitiful after Fyrn left. It was as if he had taken all her mojo with him. She hadn't even been able to summon the shield again.

Ugh.

Styx sat on her head eating a tiny piece of apple, which was all Bertha would agree to feed him. As Victoria peeled off small pieces of apple and lifted them to his tiny hands, she occasionally snuck a bite of her own. One elvish woman in a regal gold gown gasped in horror at the sight of Victoria sticking an apple slice in her mouth.

"Sorry, I should share." Victoria flashed a fake smile and threw the slice at the elf's gown. It bounced once on the cobblestone at her feet. The woman huffed and, chin raised, stormed off down the street.

These people were crazy. Apples tasted great.

Victoria bit into another apple slice, watching Main

Street. Throngs of people passed Bertha's shop, all of them pausing at one point or another to watch her, to observe and study the strange human in their midst. Bit by bit she was learning the various creatures here—goblins, ogres, elves. It seemed as though a new type of creature walked by every minute, sometimes on four legs. This was truly a mecca for all kinds of beings.

All kinds except hers.

She wondered why she stood out. In the scheme of things, a wizard or witch looked exactly like a human, at least to her. When she had met Fyrn, he had seemed like any other old man she'd ever met in her life, save for the stereotypical beard, staff, and wizard's hat. Seriously, that thing was comical. And yet, everyone stared at her as though she had three heads.

She paused, scanning the crowd once more. Though she saw elves, many of whom had similar skin tones to humans, there weren't that many witches or wizards here. Even if she were a witch, she would likely stand out like a sore thumb.

Finally done with the apple, she tossed the core into a trash bin by the door and set her palms on the corners of the crate. She was waiting for customers, someone to come by and pay for goods with the little crystals everyone exchanged here. The money, the neighbors, even the light —nothing here was like home. Although she was still on Earth, it felt as if she had traveled to another planet entirely, one where she barely knew anything about the people or their rules. Her heart sank—she was over-whelmed, with no idea where the strangeness would end. *If* it would end. Her only choice was to get used to it, to learn the language and customs of this new place, at least until she could kill Luak and go home.

Her jaw tensed as she remembered the house that had burned to ashes with her parents inside. Even though she had been caught up in the moment earlier today with Fyrn, it was true that she didn't have a home anymore.

She scanned the street once more, taking in the four- and five-story houses crammed next to each other in the main thoroughfare. The bustling heads bobbed as they wove through the crowds, everyone trying to get somewhere in this city she knew almost nothing about. Neck craning, she studied the giant crystal stalactite overhead, which miraculously eased her panic somewhat. The beautiful crystal radiated light, a soothing glow that illuminated the cavern and gave her a sliver of peace.

She cautiously set her hand on the artifact in her arm, still hidden as it was beneath her long-sleeved shirt. If she were being honest, the truth was simple: she didn't like not having control, and now she didn't even have control of her own body. This Rhazdon Artifact summoned swords and shields and even healed her. It changed the way she saw the world in both the literal and figurative senses, and she had no say in any of it. She didn't need to think about the future or what was waiting for her back in Seattle since she was having a hard enough time keeping up with the present.

After her little spat with Fyrn, it had become abundantly clear that she needed a powerful ally. Someone—anyone—who could teach her about this Rhazdon Artifact that had fused with her.

"Four bundles of bamboo and a bag of plits," a gruff voice said.

She snapped out of her reverie to find a goblin standing in front of her, only about four feet tall but as wide as the doorway. His pointed ears ended a good two feet higher than his head, and had several symmetrical notches in them. They flapped while he spoke, like wings that would never take him anywhere. His squat face reminded Victoria a bit of a frog, with a flat nose and a wrinkly scowl.

"I'm sorry, sir, what was that?"

He snorted, and a puff of smoke shot out of his nose. "Four bundles of bamboo and a bag of plits!"

Plits. Shit. She scanned the crates of fruits and vegetables in front of her, reaching for the bamboo as a diversion while she tried to remember what the hell a plit was. Bertha had given them a rundown of all the fruits and vegetables, but there were at least twenty that Victoria had never seen before in her life. Apparently the food they grew in the caves and farms in Fairhaven was unlike any in the world above, and they seemed hell-bent on using the weirdest fucking names ever.

A plit. Plit. She had used some kind of memorization trick for this one—plit, peach, plink, like metal. Right! A silver peach. She reached for the crate, shoveling six into a small bag hidden in the corner. They squished a little under her touch, as though they were weak, hollow shells filled with water.

"One denni, per usual," Bertha said from behind.

Victoria spun on her heel, relieved that Bertha had intervened. The ogre had promised to step in when money was involved, but the sensation of an impatient, waiting customer reminded Victoria of the times when, as a kid, her mom would leave her in the checkout line to go get something she had forgotten—the tension, the nerves, not being able to pay and the fear of holding up the line.

The goblin grumbled something unintelligible, and Bertha chuckled under her breath. It was likely an insult in another language, but Victoria didn't care what some grumpy old gremlin thought of her. She pretended to busy herself rearranging the plits.

As she knelt to retrieve one that had fallen to the ground, something hovered in her periphery. It was the tiniest goblin she had ever seen—probably no more than two and half feet tall, with pink bows tied around the base of her thin ears. She smiled, her face wrinkling and her ears flapping a little bit as she handed Victoria a blue flower with a glowing pink center.

Victoria smiled, still kneeling as she accepted the flower. "It's beautiful. Thank you."

The girl giggled and ran after the larger goblin, who must have been her father. Victoria studied the flower, her nerves settling somewhat at the small act of kindness. She stuck it behind her ear.

Audrey walked outside, the steps creaking underneath her as she brought out a crate of blue bananas. "Do you have an admirer already? Jeez, save some for me."

Victoria grinned. "Just a very nice little girl."

Audrey set down the crates with a huff and dusted off her hands. "Well, that's—"

"Thief! My bag! S-someone help!"

"Huh?" Victoria scanned the crowd. A hole had formed

around an elvish woman. Her yellow gown spilled over the cobblestones, her massive sleeve hanging from a thin wrist as she pointed toward the castle. It didn't take long to find what she was pointing at—another elf raced through the crowd, a hood over his head as he pushed past people and knocked others over crates.

Victoria didn't hesitate. She took off after him, keeping to the edges of the crowd so she could run faster. Sure enough, several people in the crowd had slowed him down, and every time he threw his shoulder into one of them he lost a bit of momentum. Victoria, on the other hand, caught up fairly quickly.

This was where her kickboxing skills finally became useful. She grinned, excited at the prospect of a fight after being without her classes since beginning their little adventure. Kickboxing had been a form of therapy that she desperately needed to return to soon.

As she neared the thief, she ducked into the crowd, eager to find gaps between the bodies wherever she could. It didn't take long. In seconds, she had tackled him. The crowd parted, giving them space. He swung, his hook missing her face by inches. She pinned his arm to the ground and socked him in the nose. He lost his grip on the leather bag, its metal latch clinking as it hit the ground. She stood, allowing just enough space between them to bring her leg back and drop her knee into his stomach. He doubled over, gasping for air. She cocked a fist, ready to throw another blow if she had to, but he stumbled to his feet and bolted into the crowd.

Victoria debated going after him, but she didn't see the

point. He had dropped the bag, and that was really all that mattered.

Careful to make sure nothing had fallen out in the tussle, Victoria grabbed the bag and jogged back to the elf who had raised all the commotion in the first place. The elf paced in front of a store, her yellow dress like a beacon guiding Victoria, and smiled a bit as their eyes met. She bowed her head, muttering something in a language Victoria didn't understand.

"Your bag," Victoria said, handing the leather satchel over.

"Ah, English. Thank you," the elf said, smiling broadly as she gently set the handbag's strap over her shoulder. She placed her hands on Victoria's cheeks and pulled her close, until she and the elf were almost nose to nose. Confused and a little uncomfortable, Victoria tensed. But that was all she did. With another small nod of her head, the elf disappeared into the bustling crowd.

"Very good, very good," a man said. Someone patted her shoulder, and Victoria found an ogre behind her who was even bigger than Bertha. He smiled, the wrinkles in his face exaggerated by his large nose.

She headed back to Bertha's stand, and nearly everyone she passed patted her on the back or nodded approvingly in her direction. Her cheeks burned with embarrassment, but she nodded and said thank you where she could. As Victoria approached Bertha's shop, the great big ogre grinned broadly.

Audrey smirked next to her, a look of approval and pride on her face. "Ya done good."

Victoria laughed. "My head is going to explode if I get any more embarrassed. I just did what anyone would do."

Bertha shook her head. "That purse would have been gone if you weren't here. Audrey tried to help you as well, but I figured I needed her more. You look like you've been in a fight or two."

"Just on the mat in practice." On the ground by the plits, Victoria spotted the blue flower the goblin girl had given her. She picked it up, examining it to make sure it hadn't been trampled.

Bertha shrugged. "Regardless, that brand of kindness won't be forgotten around here. You just made some friends, Victoria. In fact—"

"What?"

"Hmm. Yes. You both may have potential." Bertha held her chin in her fingers, scanning them.

Audrey crossed her arms. "Cryptic much?"

"Fairhaven is known for its food, but we also play a mean game of Berserk. I think you would both do well on my brother's team."

Victoria laughed. She couldn't help it. "Do we even want to know what that is?"

"A fun game, I assure you. I'll speak with him and see if he needs more players."

Audrey leaned in, voice a whisper. "Is that a good idea? You shouldn't be around people, much less in a game called "Berserk.'"

Victoria's smile faded. "You're probably right. Let's play it by ear. Maybe you could have some fun, though, if the game looks like something you'd enjoy."

"Ugly but good-natured," Bertha said under her breath.

The ogre apparently hadn't heard them as she lumbered up the stairs into her shop, smiling.

"Seriously, she needs stop calling us ugly," Audrey said under her breath.

Victoria shook her head, laughing, and once more tucked the little blue flower behind her ear.

CHAPTER FIFTEEN

Their evening shift at Bertha's finally over, Audrey sat in Victoria's training cave, no longer bothering to keep an eye out for the old wizard since he had been able to surprise her last time. Part of her wondered if he would turn them in, but common sense said he wouldn't. If he had wanted to, he would have already. Instead of worrying she watched Victoria train, and it wasn't going well.

Styx sat on Audrey's shoulder, and they had both spent most of the last hour wincing as Victoria hurt herself in increasingly colorful ways.

With a large gash across her cheek from her last run-in with the shield, Victoria spread her feet in a sparring stance and lifted her right arm as if she were waiting for a falcon to land on it. The awkward pose had created the best results so far, though that was admittedly a generous way to phrase it. Audrey wondered what her buddy would try to summon this time—not that it really mattered. The shield and the sword seemed to appear with equal irregularity.

Victoria frowned, her expression painfully serious she focused on her arm. Her breathing slowed, and the cave went silent. Audrey leaned forward, holding her breath as she waited to see what would happen. Maybe this time, Victoria would finally—

A shield twice the size of Victoria's body appeared out of thin air, completely blocking her from Audrey's view. The coppery metal embedded itself in the rock wall, rooting the shield in place. Audrey flinched, caught off-guard, but Victoria let out a string of curse words that would make any sailor blush.

"She's quite terrible at this," Shiloh said, appearing out of nowhere behind Audrey.

Audrey jumped a good foot in the air at his sudden appearance, hand on her heart she glared at him. "Stop doing that!"

He stared at her, his bored features unfazed by her outburst.

She grunted exasperation. "It freaks me out when you appear without warning. Every. Damn. Time."

"I'm astonished that you think I care," he said, leaning against the cave's rocky wall.

Audrey crossed her arms, giving him a once-over. "You could at least be useful and go help her."

"Nah."

Victoria fumbled and fell on her ass, still struggling with the shield and apparently unable to put it away.

In an instant he had disappeared, leaving only Audrey, Victoria, and Styx in the otherwise empty cave.

What a stupid jerk.

Victoria's shield disappeared. Apparently caught off-guard, Victoria fell backward onto the rocky floor once again, her head smacking hard against the ground. Teeth biting her lip, she sucked in a sharp breath and cradled the back of her skull. "Fuuuuuuuck!"

"Victoria! Are you—"

"Screw this bullshit!" Victoria leapt to her feet and stormed out of the cave, blowing past Audrey without a sideways glance. Styx flitted after Victoria, hovering just out of reach.

Audrey grimaced, giving her friend the space she obviously needed, but she had seen this once before. Victoria had faced off with a much more advanced kickboxer who had been too rough with her in one of their first classes. It was the kind of anger that burned bright and hot, and the only way to help was to back off. Victoria would be fine once she walked off the pain.

As the sound of Victoria's stomping feet retreated, Audrey sat on one of the boulders by the cave's entrance. Elbows on her knees, hands intertwined, she stared at the palace in Fairhaven's center. It was a beautiful building, and probably nice to live in. Sure, Audrey wasn't one for frills and gold, but she could still appreciate the finer things. Maybe someday they could take a tour or something to see how the other half lived here in Fairhaven.

It would probably be a good hour or two until Victoria calmed down, and because they were in a foreign city, Victoria would stay close to home. She could be hot-headed, but she wasn't an idiot. She didn't need a babysitter.

As the light from the crystal overhead began to dim, Audrey left the cave as well. Hands in her pockets, she walked through the crowds in the busy streets of Fairhaven, sticking to the areas she remembered but otherwise letting her feet take her wherever they wanted to go.

She passed rows and rows of shops, but she didn't bother window shopping. Given their predicament, it was best not to have a lot of things. Traveling light would make it easier to disappear if they needed to.

The ground began to slope upward, and the dimming light of Fairhaven faded behind her. She blinked herself out of her daze, panicking for a moment as she wondered if she had traveled too far.

Main Street was behind her. Somehow she had walked right by Bertha's shop without even noticing. She studied the cobblestones and glanced around.

Wait, she knew this trail. This was the path that led back up to the bridge they had used to enter the city. She hesitated on the empty path, wondering why her feet would take her here.

Perhaps, deep down, she wanted to leave.

She had never let herself consider that option, since she would never abandon Victoria. Not in a million years, no matter what she really wanted to do. But deep down, Audrey missed home. She spun on her heel and was treated to another breathtaking view of Fairhaven, her eyes lingering here and there on the stranger things—the tilting homes, the ogres, the elves. She leaned against the wall, taking it all in. And there, a constant backdrop to it all, was the massive white palace in the middle.

The city, the streets, and the bobbing heads below her were unlike anything she'd ever seen or experienced in her life. Magic. Power. Astounding creatures that hardly seemed possible.

As much as she might want to go home and have normalcy once more, Audrey could never go back to her old life. Not really. What did strip malls and grocery stores offer compared to this? The human world didn't even come close.

She reached into her pocket and pulled out her phone, which she had powered down during their first descent into the city. She tapped her thumb against it, wondering if her parents were awake. It was hard to keep track of time in Fairhaven, since she hadn't seen the sun in almost a week.

She turned it on and held her breath as she waited for the battery bar to appear.

53%

Good. Unsure of what to say, her throat a bit dry with nerves, she pressed autodial and set the phone against her ear, fingers straining as she pushed it against her head.

The ringing stopped, and the line crackled. A faint voice answered. "Hello?"

"Mom! It's good to hear your voice."

"Oh, you, too, sweetie! How's the road trip? How's Victoria?"

Audrey cleared her throat. "She's, uh, hurting. Doing her best, as always."

"Such a tough cookie."

Now for the lie. Audrey's mouth went dry from guilt, but she forced herself through it. "We're thinking about backpacking through Europe, Asia, you name it. We might be gone for a while, and we won't have cell reception through most of it."

"Well, don't die."

Audrey laughed. "Great advice as always, Mom."

"I try."

Audrey smiled, more grateful than she had realized she would be to hear her mother's voice. "Is Dad home too?"

"Sure is. He's tinkering in the garage. Hold on, I'll go get him." The line crackled some more, and for a moment Audrey was worried the call would drop. A second later, though, the sound of a door creaking open on a noisy hinge came over the line, followed by the whirring buzz of a saw.

Audrey kicked little pebbles on the path as she waited for her dad to join the conversation. Her cheeks hurt, and it took a moment to realize it was because she was smiling. She didn't want to say it around Victoria, but Victoria's parents' death had made Audrey even more grateful for her own family. It was easy to forget that they could be gone in a flash, and she had to confess she sometimes took them for granted. But right now, she wanted to hear every story, get every update—everything. She would talk either until they hung up or her phone went dead.

To be honest, Victoria had no fucking clue where she was.

The closely-knit houses and tightly packed streets had disappeared about twenty minutes ago, and Victoria now walked along a dirt path she didn't recognize. In her fury, she had ignored the path for too long and ended up somewhere strange without the faintest clue of how she'd gotten here. With every step her anger faded, replaced instead by exhaustion and frustration. She wanted to cry and scream and take a nap all at once, but none of those would help her. Complaining wouldn't do any good either. Not even venting her anger would help her understand the magic in her arm any better.

She needed to focus. She needed to be calm.

In the dimming light of the massive crystal overhead, she paused in the street, taking a deep breath to clear her mind and reacquaint herself with her surroundings. Only a handful of ogres walked on the road, and by some miracle most of them ignored her. They carried baskets filled with turnips and onions, and the houses around here all had little yards with rocky paths and two-foot-tall rock walls. A few even had circles of mushrooms growing in the front yards, which reminded Victoria of her childhood walks through parks and streams. A bunch of mushrooms like that was called a fairy circle, and humans like her weren't supposed to walk through one or the fae would grab them and steal them away.

Victoria laughed at the old wives' tale, but her smile quickly faded. Today she had chased an elf and sold fruit to a goblin. Fairies were probably real too, so she wasn't about to test her luck.

These buildings shifted and breathed, creaking a little as they rocked very gently from side to side. It was as if they were trees in a breeze, trembling a little in a gust she couldn't feel.

The sound of water caught her attention, and she followed it to a little path that broke off from the main road. The gravel trail wound through some trees, the first forest she had seen since coming to Fairhaven, and ended at a small waterfall. Thick moss and lichen covered the rock, offering a bit of reprieve to her bruised bum as she sat down. It compressed beneath her like memory foam, and she smiled at the relaxing feeling.

She trailed her hand in the water, the ripples glowing blue at her touch. She grinned. There was nothing like this above ground. True, the people here were weird and kept calling her ugly, but if she had to be honest, she adored them all and the city they lived in. Perhaps when this was all over, she would find a place here and stay.

Alone in this little grove, Victoria lifted her sleeve slightly to reveal the artifact underneath. Even just looking at it triggered a flurry of emotions: anger, fear, bloodlust.

Out of nowhere, the shield appeared once more, slicing through the mossy bank and embedding itself in the rock beneath. Furious, frustrated, and so fucking done with the nonsense, she cursed so loudly her voice echoed.

CHAPTER SIXTEEN

As the light from the crystals overhead began to fade, Victoria remained by her little waterfall somewhere on the outskirts of Fairhaven. She had no idea how much time had passed, and part of her didn't care. Besides, she had no idea where she was or how to get back to a familiar part of town. That was Audrey's superpower, not hers. Perhaps it would be better to stay the night by this waterfall, since it seemed safe and isolated enough. Besides, the longer she sat by the flowing water and the more time she spent running her hand through the glowing blue stream, the more she fell in love with this strange city filled with magical creatures.

But as darkness crept into the city, a chill settled into her skin. It was deep and cold, the kind of bite that clings to the body after getting out of a pool. In the last rays of the crystals' light, she could see the puffs of her breath freeze in the air. Strange. She and Audrey had been fine in the cave, but maybe the tiny space and the shared body heat had kept it warm enough to sleep in. Out here, it seemed cold enough to snow.

She shivered, rubbing her arms to keep herself warm, but Plan A wouldn't work. Somehow, she needed to get back to Bertha's shop. How she would manage it, she didn't know.

Her best bet would be to head back toward Fyrn's, since she could at least camp out in the cave again until morning. After all, she couldn't be too far away. The crystals overhead still produced a gentle glow like twilight that illuminated just enough to still see without being able to read by it. Even though the walls of the massive cavern all looked the same, the glowing center crystal overhead had unique wrinkles and dips in it. From this angle, it looked distinctly different than she was used to, meaning she was far from home.

The palace stretched toward the cavern's ceiling, this side of its tallest tower identical to the other except for a balcony she had never seen before. That probably meant she was on the other side of the city from where she should be.

Awesome.

Okay, Plan C: hike toward the palace, pass it, and find herself back on Main Street. Easy enough.

Groaning, annoyed with herself, she started the long trek home. As she walked, doing her best to keep her path headed toward the castle whenever the lighted pathways would allow her to, she continued to rub the non-metallic parts of her arms to keep herself warm. A chill leapt from the embedded dagger as her thumb brushed it, and she shivered. Her long-sleeved shirt wasn't enough in the growing cold. She and Audrey would need to do some shopping.

Step by step, road by road, she neared the castle as the crystals' light continued to fade. It was nearly pitch-black, with only the gentlest glow from the overhead crystals emulating moonlight. Streetlights filled with tiny flames lit some of the roads, casting yellow light over the cobblestone paths before her. Fewer and fewer people walked past her in the streets, and Victoria kept her eyes peeled for trouble. Talk about having a bullseye on her back: a girl, alone, walking through dimly lit streets in the middle of the night? Nothing suspicious about that. She scanned every alley, every porch, every shadow for danger.

She turned a corner to find two elves leaning against the wall, each smoking a pipe. Their eyes shifted toward her and lingered, barely blinking as she passed. Not one to back down, she made eye contact with both to drive home the fact that she had seen them, narrowing her eyes a bit to add a touch of challenge to their persistent gazes. Even as she continued down the street out of reach, she could feel their eyes on the back of her neck.

The castle grew massive and continuously closer. Its white walls towered overhead, easily thirty feet high. A guard in a metal helmet and armor walked along the top, surveying the ground below. The castle itself loomed, almost impossibly large. In fact, she would bet the entire population could fit inside if crammed closely enough together. Perhaps that was the point—a stronghold if the city were ever attacked. Once she passed it, she should have a straight shot back to Bertha's house.

Almost home.

A massive ogre lumbered into the street to her left, appearing almost out of nowhere. He growled softly, his eyes focused squarely on her. With his massive teeth, he bit into a raw hunk of meat. Blood splattered into the air.

"Whoa!" Victoria jumped out of the way seconds before the spray could reach her. Spooked, her nerves already on edge from the elves she had passed earlier, she jumped back into a fighting stance on instinct, lifting her right arm to shield her body.

On its own, the shield appeared in her hand. For the first time ever, it was the right size.

But she had summoned it in company. Her secret was out.

The ogre jumped a good two feet in the air and ran back into the alley like a frightened field mouse, his pants falling to his ankles as he sped off.

"Go away," she muttered to the shield, shaking her wrist to make it vanish. Terrified, Victoria looked at the palace walls. No guards. No one on the empty street. The firelight flickered in one of the lamps further down the road, but the one over her head wasn't even lit.

The shield disappeared, and she regained control of her hand. Allowing herself a sigh of relief, she walked at a brisker pace toward the palace.

"I know what you are," a deep, gruff voice said.

She spun on her heel, jumping into a fighting stance again as an elf with broad shoulders and a barrel chest walked out of the alley across the street. He stood a good foot taller than any of the elves she had seen so far, and had a cigar in his mouth and a scar over his right eye. His long black hair fell in dreadlocks to his lower back, and he sneered at her.

"Hosts are not allowed in Fairhaven," he said, spitting out the cigar in his mouth. It fizzled on the ground, a thin stream of smoke rising from the tip.

Victoria lifted her fists. In kickboxing class, her teacher always told her not to get into a fighting stance if threatened because it ruined the element of surprise. Most muggers wouldn't assume their victim knew how to fight. But here, now, Victoria didn't bother with pretense. If he really did know what she was, he wouldn't underestimate her.

Shit.

He lifted his hand, still a good twenty feet away, and fiery symbols appeared on the back. He narrowed his eyes, which glowed as his gaze focused squarely on her.

Oh, right. This place had magic—real magic, not just Rhazdon Artifacts. She wouldn't just be in a fistfight, not down here. Every fight had a new element to consider, likely more dangerous than any gun.

Double shit.

A blast of yellow light sailed toward her. Thanks to her quick reflexes, she tucked and rolled to get out of the way. The beam singed her sleeve. The embers of the burning fibers scorched her skin, and she patted them quickly to put them out. She wasn't given much time to put together a game plan, though. He shot another blast of light at her, and she once more had to duck.

Screw this. It was time to go on the offensive.

Without much of a plan or any experience with combat magic, Victoria didn't wait for him to reload his magic slingshot—or whatever the hell he was doing. She charged. The glowing symbols faded as he braced himself for impact and dug his heel into the road, placing his hands out to grab her as she neared.

Like hell. She wasn't an idiot.

At the last second, she feinted to the left and kneed him as hard as she could in the stomach. A violent huff of air escaped him, and he collapsed to his hands and knees. Weight on the balls of her feet, she pivoted her left foot and landed a roundhouse kick on his head.

A thin spatter blood left his mouth as he went down, and Victoria jumped out of contact so that he couldn't grab her while she figured out what to do next.

His skin began to glow again, but this time he glared at her with an expression of hatred she had only seen in movies.

This fucker wanted to straight-up *kill* her.

The frustrated, angry, vengeful part of her didn't care. Bring it. Whatever. That hateful slice of her brain wanted to rip into him, to finally let loose all her resentment at not being able to control the Rhazdon Artifact embedded in her arm. Now, when she needed it most, the damn thing refused to appear. Just like the ghost attached to it, the dagger wouldn't listen to her, wouldn't obey, and she was sick of fighting it.

And yet...

And yet the rational, intelligent, capable survivalist within her knew better. Yeah, she could fight, but she hadn't studied many martial arts—just kickboxing, and that was mostly for fitness and fun. Sure, she had a mean knee and a killer roundhouse, but this was officially the first fight she had ever been in. Based on his glare and the scar on his face, this elf had been in far more.

She knew when to retreat to live another day.

Fast as lightning, she raced down the street, searing blasts hitting the road on either side of her as she dodged, the magical attacks kicking up cobblestones and dust as she ran. The elf charged after her, his powerful legs slightly faster than hers.

He was catching up.

"Shit," she said under her breath. Thanks to the way everything seemed to be going wrong, the word was quickly becoming her mantra.

In the growing darkness, a little white orb appeared directly ahead of her. It floated, dancing like a wisp in a swamp. She slowed, debating her options, not quite sure which was her bigger problem.

The blip of light began to grow, becoming as large as a basketball and then as large as a car. She skidded to a halt, lifting her arm to protect her eyes as the wisp overtook everything around it.

When the light receded, the path was almost pitch black. Every lantern had been blown out, and the only surviving light was the faint glow from the crystals over-head. A silhouette stood near her in the darkness, wearing a ridiculous hat and holding a familiar staff.

Fyrn.

He tapped his walking stick against the road, and the first detail she could make out on his face was a withering scowl. But—for the first time—he wasn't scowling at *her*. He studied the street over her shoulder, where a figure lay in one of the half-dozen grooves the elf's magic had dug into the road. Bit by bit, Victoria's eyes adjusted to the darkness. The elf lifted his head and, to her horror, his eyes were entirely white, irises gone. Babbling incoherently and drooling a little, he rolled onto his back and stared at the green crystals overhead.

"We need to go," Fyrn said. He walked toward a side-street, beckoning her to follow with a wave of his hand.

She trotted next to him, constantly looking over her shoulder at the elf now lying on the ground in the middle of an obliterated street. "What did you do to him?"

"He's fine."

"That's cool and all, but what did you do? He knows what I am. If he—"

"He won't remember."

"Look, thank you for what you did, but *come on*! If you're always going to play the cryptic wizard who says vague shit and doesn't give me any answers, we're not going to get along."

"I erased his memory."

Sweet. She grinned, curious. "You can really do that?"

"I just did."

"What about anyone in their homes? If they overheard—"

"In that neighborhood, no one overhears anything if they want to live a long and healthy life." He looked at her over the bridge of his nose, frowning in disappointment.

Ah. She'd gone to the wrong part of town. "Sorry."

"Are you *trying* to get yourself killed?"

"Not trying. I'm just good at it."

He groaned, rubbing his temples as he turned down a second alley. "Don't worry about anyone who overheard.

That spell works within a hundred-foot radius, through windows. It only affects memories that happened a few moments before I trigger the spell, so it's limited. If anyone witnessed or heard what happened, they have already forgotten. Unless, of course, someone was watching out of reach of my spell."

"Is that possible?"

He paused and looked over his shoulder, catching her eye. "Someone is always watching in Fairhaven."

Her jaw tensed. "Good to know."

With a slight limp to his step, he led her onto another street, this one better lit and with nicer cobblestones than the road where she had been attacked.

"You need a proper map," he said.

"Bertha drew one for me. I just forgot it at—"

"A proper map. A real one. You must keep it on you always. I'll mark the areas to avoid, especially someone like you." He stared at her as if to drive his point home.

She frowned, putting her hands on her hips and stopping in the middle of the empty street. "Someone like—look, why do you even care?"

He paused, settling his weight against the staff as he studied her with a bored expression. "Explain."

"You've been telling me to leave since I got here. Why did you save me?"

"You're welcome." He carried on, leading the way through the unfamiliar street.

Victoria sighed, exasperated, and caught up to him. For an old guy, he sure set a brisk pace. "Thank you again for what you did back there. I appreciate your help, I do, but it's a fair question to ask. I need to know I can trust you, and right now you're just confusing me. After all, you've been a bit of an ass up to this point."

He grinned as if pleased with himself. "I have, haven't I?"

"Yeah, majorly."

"And yet you stayed."

"Well, yeah. I didn't have a choice."

He rolled his eyes. "Heroes! You're all the same. Of course you had a choice, Victoria. Any sane human being would have left. She would have gone home, or gone to live on a mountain in the woods and pretended nothing had happened, that she had never been to a magical city called Fairhaven or seen ogres or packaged plits for goblins."

Realization crashed through Victoria. "You've been watching me. That's how you knew about Bertha."

He nodded, lowering his voice. "You're a host in my city. Of course I've been watching you."

She bit her cheek to keep from saying something stupid. "Fine. What did you discover as you stalked me?"

"You have heart."

Confused, squinting a little as she tried to make sense of the statement, she shrugged. "What?"

"You've helped many people here, and you do it for no reason other than because you care. You chased down that thief, put yourself in harm's way to recover a stranger's purse. You help that ogre with her shop, even though you have a large pouch of denni on you."

"How did you—"

"You're not nearly as covert as you should be. It's dumb luck a thief hasn't tried to snatch it. Never fear, I'll teach you stealth."

"Hey, I'm plenty stealthy."

"Hardly." He laughed, a single huff of air that reminded Victoria of a car backfiring.

What a grumpy old man. She frowned, pretending to study the buildings they passed. The buildings were straighter here, with nicer trim and elegant iron gates protecting their tiny moss yards.

"I suppose I can't hate you for your parents," he said softly.

She glared at him, but he didn't flinch. He didn't even look at her. He stared ahead, a wistful look on his face as his eyes slipped out of focus.

He paused, both hands on the staff as he leaned on it. "In the morning, you will quit your job. You will train with me for at least ten hours every day. Those are my terms, and should you fail to meet my expectations, I will no longer teach you. I am unpleasant, rude, and unfair, but this is life and death, Victoria. I'll train you. I'll show you what it means to be"—he lowered his voice, leaning in—"a host. I believe that is what you came for, wasn't it?"

She stood a bit taller. Damn right it was. "Unpleasant, rude, or unfair, I don't mind. Show me what you've got. I'm ready."

CHAPTER SEVENTEEN

Flames crackling over his skin, Luak stepped out of the burning farmhouse onto the tattered remnants of the wraparound front porch. In his hand he held a Dragon amulet, yet another Rhazdon Artifact he could return to his master. He didn't even know what this one did, but it didn't matter. He had recovered it from yet another clueless human who had stuck his nose into something that didn't concern him. After all, Oriceran magic belonged to those with magical blood, not these magicless creatures who wasted air.

True, he had seen humans wielding magic on occasion, but human magic was inferior to the power of those with Oriceran blood. And of all the Oriceran creatures, Light Elves were the most impressive. He grinned with pride.

A support beam collapsed, taking the roof with it. A wave of hot air shattered the windows, and he briefly closed his eyes to shield them from the shards. He studied the burning farmhouse as he mentally checked off the corpses inside—the mother and father hadn't known what was happening, but the adult son had. Luak didn't know where the twenty-something young man had found a Rhazdon Artifact, but he had brought dark magic into his parents' home without their knowledge. It was his fault he and his parents were now dead.

Any sane human would leave Oriceran magic alone.

Black smoke billowed into the sky as the farmhouse burned. Three brown horses thundered in circles in a nearby pen, panicked by the flames and running in circles to avoid a danger that wasn't even a minor threat to them.

Idiot creatures. Not unlike humans.

Content, Luak returned to the black SUV he had rented after the flight to Montana, his precious Rhazdon Artifact in hand. His master would be pleased that he had returned another one, but he had only just begun to serve. Fairhaven was next, and once he took the city, he would forever have a seat at the table of his master's inner circle.

It would be a long drive back to the airport, but he could spend it deciding which law to enact first upon becoming king: either all would kneel every time he entered a room, or the citizens would bring a tribute of their finest dishes on the first of every month. Perhaps he would hold a gala where the young elvish women of Fairhaven could compete to become one of his brides.

His grip on the wheel tightened. Being king would be so much *fun*.

CHAPTER EIGHTEEN

Victoria settled onto a couch in the middle of Fyrn's living room. As she sat, a puff of dust spewed from the cushions and caught in her lungs, gagging her. Evidently he didn't entertain much.

The small cottage expanded infinitely once she walked inside, every room connected by a long hallway that seemed to stretch on forever. The living room itself, however, didn't have a single clean surface. Every table and bookshelf, and even the floor, was covered in books, scrolls, and journals. Coffee mugs and glass cups were filled with quills and an occasional pen from a human hotel. The juxtaposition of his world and hers in a single cup was surreal, as if she would wake up any moment from this crazy roller coaster of a dream.

"You want answers," Fyrn said, collapsing into the armchair across from her. He snapped his fingers, and his staff grew four tiny legs. It walked itself to the bookshelf and leaned against it as he laced his fingers together and set his hands on his chest.

"Answers would be nice, yes," she said, eyes still lingering on the self-propelled walking stick.

He nodded, frowning a little. He must've been wondering where to start. "Do you know the word 'Oriceran?'"

She sat upright. "It was written on a notebook my mom and dad left for me, but I don't really know what it is."

"Oriceran is an entirely different world in a dimension very similar to ours, and every twenty-five thousand and eight hundred years, Oriceran and Earth rotate close enough that the veil between the two becomes thin. Gates open between the two worlds, kind of like enormous doors. The magic from Oriceran flows into Earth until there's equilibrium. As we speak, the natural gates between the worlds are very slowly opening. This will continue over the next millennium until the creatures from both worlds mix with each other. The last time it happened, the resulting culture clash caused unspeakable war and destruction. There's talk in Fairhaven of both worlds looking for ways to get ready this time, some of it with good intentions.

"But it's so early in the cycle that trying to create a portal, a much smaller temporary door, is dangerous and can lead to death or worse. It's illegal to magically manipulate portals into opening early, but some do it anyway. The willens are particularly gifted at it."

She opened her mouth to ask the inevitable question, but he held a hand up to stop her. "Willens are rodents that walk on two legs and talk. They're petty thieves and very clever at stealing not only shiny objects, but also secrets.

Somehow they've figured out a better way to open a portal with less risk."

"Wait, wait," Victoria pinched the bridge of her nose as she absorbed all this information. "All the creatures in Fairhaven are from another world?"

"We are, yes. Our ancestors stayed on Earth, choosing to hide themselves from humans to avoid a second great war."

"Jesus."

"Indeed. In fact, that dagger embedded in your arm was created on Oriceran."

She marveled at the metal artifact. "This was created on another world?"

"It was. As I mentioned before, that dagger in your arm is called a Rhazdon Artifact. It's a dangerous blend of dark magic and death that has been banned in every magical city I know of, both on Earth and on Oriceran. In fact, on Oriceran, all known Rhazdon Artifacts are locked away in an enormous vault in a library kept and protected by the Gnomes. The Rhazdon Artifact feeds off you, drawing its power from your life force and energy. In exchange, it gives you magical capabilities unlike anything else in our world. As far as I know, no two Rhazdon Artifacts are alike —every single one has different powers. Some even enhance you, make you stronger and, in some cases, smarter. However, judging by your decisions thus far, I'm pretty sure you don't have that one."

"Har, har."

He grinned, the first genuine smile she had ever seen on his face. "Victoria, what powers does yours give you?"

"It's a little hard to tell, since I can't really control them.

I know it can create a shield, a sword, and a dagger. It heals me, at least I think it does. I've had some pretty bad wounds since this fused to me, and I've walked away without a scratch every time. I was also able to see through the spell around your house. Audrey couldn't see your cottage, but I could."

"Damn. No, that's not the Artifact, at least not entirely. The bubble is an experimental spell, and the fact you could see through it probably has more to do with what I need to do to improve the spell than the magic in your arm. Let's dismiss that until we can study it further."

"Okay. Healing, shield, sword, dagger. That seems to be it, at least so far."

Fyrn tapped his index fingers together, an indent appearing in his cheek as he bit it. "No, an artifact only gives three powers to its host. The healing is definitely one of them, but I think the other two are giving you the ability to summon a shield, and the ability to summon any kind of weapon you choose. In those moments, do you think of a dagger? Were you thinking of the sword?"

"Technically I didn't summon the sword. My dad did. When I summoned the dagger, I wasn't thinking about any weapon in particular, just the end goal—to kill Luak."

"Interesting. You saw your father use the Rhazdon Artifact?"

Guilt and sadness crashed through Victoria in one powerful, painful wave. She nodded and looked at the floor.

"Ah. No matter. In our training, we will explore this further and see if you can summon the sword as well. Now, there's something else you need to know. With these three powers, you must always make a choice—to use one of them to the full capacity, or to use two or three at partial power."

"I don't follow."

"If you were seriously wounded, you would not be able to summon a shield or sword if you also wanted to heal. However, if you had a flesh wound, you could devote a small amount of your power to healing it while you continue to wield a sword in one hand and shield in the other. Does that make sense?"

She nodded. "I have to be careful about how much power I allocate to each of the gifts."

"Exactly."

She hesitated, running her tongue over her back molar as she tried to figure out how she wanted to word her next question. "How do you know so much about the Rhazdon Artifacts? From everything you've said so far, being a host is a death sentence. It seems like no one has bothered to get to know the hosts, and yet here you are, offering to train me. What experience do you have with them?"

He studied her a moment, and for a little while she thought he wasn't going to answer. He sighed deeply. "I study things that others dismiss. Power, real power, lies in the cracks that others ignore. There's so much more going on here and in your world than either of us will ever know. Every new question has an answer that leads down a rabbit hole of more questions. The pursuit of magical knowledge is eternal, and I have devoted my life to studying what others fear."

"That doesn't really answer—"

"All that was to say," he interrupted, "that I know more

about most fields of study than many experts do. It is my purpose to learn and to teach, even when it comes to dark magic. It's illegal of course, but without a solid understanding of what we're up against, we can't fight it."

Victoria sat up straighter, eyes narrowing at what he had just implied. "This dark magic is fused with my body, so are you going to fight *me*? Are you just studying me to take me out later?"

"I try not to destroy what I create," he said.

Victoria tensed, not entirely certain she liked that answer.

He pointed to her arm. "Roll up your sleeve."

She frowned, unhappy at being ordered around, but she needed his help so she obeyed. The artifact glimmered in the living room's candlelight, the cogs and wheels of the steampunk dagger reminding her of an old, dismantled clock fused with a knife.

"Have you tried to pull it out?" Fyrn asked.

She shook her head. "I like being alive."

"Smart. How do you know removing it will kill you?"

"The ghost."

Fyrn clicked his tongue. "Ah, yes. I can tell you more about the ghosts later. For now, what is yours like?"

"He's a pain in the ass."

"They often are."

Victoria chuckled, not caring if Shiloh had heard. She ran a finger over the metal hilt. "Why would removing it kill me?"

Fyrn hesitated, tapping his finger on his knee. "The fusion is complete. It becomes part of you, a fundamental, necessary organ in your body. You become dependent upon it the same way it is dependent upon you, and to remove it is like removing your heart or your brain."

Victoria shuddered.

"That's part of why they're feared," Fyrn continued. "Dark magic takes more than it gives, but what it gives is powerful and absolute. Some believe the sacrifice required to wield dark magic corrupts the soul, and that you have to give up an element of who you are to use it."

"That's why a host is killed on sight," Victoria said.

Fyrn nodded. "It's that, but it's also the way the Rhazdon Artifacts are made."

"What you mean?"

"Rhazdon was a creature of great power—a terror who idolized dark magic—and only he knew how to make these dark artifacts. When Rhazdon decided he wanted to immortalize a gift he saw in another and wield it himself, he would perform a very specific ritual. To create your artifact, for instance, Rhazdon likely identified a great warrior who was legendary on the battlefield, whose skill he wanted to gain for himself. To do that, Rhazdon took something of value to that person to lure him in and then murdered the warrior to fuse his soul with the weapon. The whole process is far more complicated, of course, but that's the essence of the ritual. That's why there's a ghost tied to the artifact."

"And that's why he's a pain in the ass. He didn't choose this life," Victoria said, mortified.

"Exactly."

"That's horrible!"

"It's inhumane, true, but it gets worse."

"Of course it does."

"To fuse with an artifact, there must be death." Fyrn stared at her intently, and the gaze became a nudge in her side. He seemed to want her to share her own story.

Her throat burned, and a knot caught there as she remembered the way her father had pulled the dagger from his body and set it on her arm with his dying breath. Her voice betrayed her, and when she spoke, it came out almost to quietly to hear. "Yes, there was a death."

"Whose?"

She glared at the floor. "My dad."

Fyrn stared at her for a moment, a confused look on his face, but he seemed to realize after a moment what she was saying. "Your father sacrificed himself for you, killing himself so that you could have the Rhazdon Artifact?"

She nodded.

"Amazing." Fyrn stood, papers crinkling under his feet as he paced the cluttered living room floor.

"I think you mean horrifying," Victoria corrected.

Fyrn paused, staring at her as he processed what she had said. "Yes, I'm sure it was. I'm sure it gave you purpose. Drive. Fire."

Victoria recalled the crackling flames as Luak's magic burned down her childhood home. "You could say that."

"It gave you a reason to fight."

She nodded.

"Will you do what I tell you?"

She frowned at him, wondering where this was going.

He continued. "As your mentor, I will teach you what you need to know to master the Rhazdon Artifact in your arm. I will teach you to be the most powerful host in Fairhaven, perhaps in all the world. When you first came here, I turned you away because I have seen Rhazdon Artifacts corrupt host after host. I have seen them crumble and fall to their own greed and bloodlust, seen them destroy everything they hold dear for even a taste of more power. But you, Victoria, don't seem affected at all by the Rhazdon Artifact in your arm. That could be because of the way you received it or just because you're one of the few who can handle having dark magic in your body. But you have a gift. I can help you hone it, but you must do whatever I tell you. You must listen to me, even if you think I'm wrong."

Victoria watched him, letting the silence settle between them as she debated how to answer. Never in her life had she followed orders if she thought they were wrong. Rules only worked when they made sense; anything less was tyranny.

"I promise," she lied.

Fyrn nodded, apparently content with her answer. "We start in the morning. Over time, I'll teach you to use magic. For now, you need to learn to control the Rhazdon Artifact itself."

She perked up, curious. "Humans can wield magic?"

He shook his head. "Not all of them. Some have a mutant gene, giving them a powerful gift to use and control magic. However, it can be difficult to know who has the gene until they are close to a kemana."

"So wizards are just humans?"

He snorted. "Not even remotely. We're an entirely separate race, and a superior one at that. Every witch and wizard of merit belongs to the Order of the Silver Griffins, a society that protects magic and keeps it hidden. It's a sacred responsibility we guard with our lives."

She rolled her eyes.

From the other side of the room, he opened the door with a wave of his hand. "Go home. No detours. You know the way by now, I presume?"

She nodded. "When I got lost earlier, I just wasn't paying attention. I was so angry."

"We'll have to work on your temper, then. Meet me here at sunrise, ready to learn."

She laughed. "There's not really a sun down here."

"Old habits. You know what I mean." He smirked.

She nodded and stood. After all that had happened, she could use a good night's rest.

Victoria knocked on Bertha's door, leaning her head against the doorframe as she yearned for bed.

The entrance swung open. Audrey stood in the foyer with a panicked look on her face, and she pulled Victoria into a tight hug—so tight that Victoria could barely breathe.

"I'm fine," she managed to say, breathless.

"You scared me shitless," Audrey said, a hand on each of Victoria's shoulders as she studied her face.

"You and me both," Victoria said with a chuckle.

"What happened?"

Victoria smiled, the grin so broad it hurt her face. "I have so much to tell you."

CHAPTER NINETEEN

The next day, Victoria followed Fyrn as he led her through the city. Styx hummed beside her, lazily swerving from side to side as he flew. This early in the morning there weren't many people to watch her, a definite plus to getting up early despite the fact she had bags under her eyes. She had a deep desire to crawl up in the nearest patch of moss and go back to sleep.

The longer they walked, the fewer creatures they saw, and finally Fyrn led her to a tunnel entrance. As the light faded, the stone on the top of his walking stick began to glow. The light had a similar effect to a car's high beam, blazing the way with a brilliant ray of light. The ground began to slope downward, gently first and then steeper and steeper until she had to set her hand against the wall for balance. Despite his limp Fyrn didn't seem to have any problems, and she wondered if a spell were involved with his sudden grace. With him a bit ahead and barely a word spoken between them, Fyrn led the way through tunnel after tunnel, twisting as the route led them deep into the caves beneath Fairhaven.

Their last tunnel ended in a towering cavern with thousands of glittering green crystals embedded in the walls lighting the space. A waterfall crashed into a small lake in the corner, and moss grew on every inch of the ground. In the distance, a meadow of waist-high purple grass covered at least half of the cavern.

Fyrn spun on his heel, tapping his staff twice on the mossy ground. "Let's begin."

Victoria skidded along the moss from Fyrn's latest blow, ending up half-submerged in the purple grass. It tickled her with tiny sparks of electricity like an anemone, and she quickly rolled out of it.

Splinters of pain pulsed in her shoulder. She nursed it, wishing she had some idea how long they had been down here. Since this cave was illuminated by its own crystals, she wasn't sure if it had a sunset and sunrise. It seemed like she and Fyrn had been in the cave for days, and judging by the ache in her bones from being thrown across the cavern so many times, she was far overdue for a break.

Each magical blast reminded her of the flames that destroyed her home and singed her skin, but she swallowed hard in an effort to ignore the flashbacks. Dwelling on the past wouldn't help her now.

Her hair hung loose around her face, as most of it had come out of the ponytail she tied this morning. Her body screamed for rest, longing to simply lie down for a moment. She forced herself to her feet, swaying a little until she recovered her balance.

"We'll take a short break," Fyrn said, giving her a once-over. Styx, hovering beside the wizard, peeked through his hands and nodded in agreement.

Victoria shook her head. She hadn't come this far to take breaks. Luak certainly wouldn't rest, and she had a long way to go to catch up to him. She could stomach a little pain. It was worth it.

"No. Again," she said, settling into her stance as she prepared once more to summon a shield. Hopefully this time it would work.

Fyrn's lips curved in the barest hint of a smile. "Very well."

As he had instructed, Victoria tensed her right arm and imagined a small shield hanging from her hand. She took measured breaths, focusing all her energy and attention toward creating the metal disc. This time a warm, tingling sensation shot through her arms, and weight pressed against her palm. She peeked through one eye to find herself holding a small version of her shield, barely the size of her head.

Her heart leapt with joy, but she didn't let her focus waiver. She studied the exposed Rhazdon Artifact, trying to figure out where the metal had come from, to understand at least *something* about the dark magic in her arm. The shield's handle didn't seem to be attached to the artifact at all.

As her attention faded, the shield flickered and dissolved into the air, disappearing entirely a mere minute after it had been summoned. Still, that was longer than she had managed to hold it thus far.

Something hit her square in the chest, shooting her backward into the purple grass. Landing hard on her shoulder blades, she couldn't stem the stream of curse words that escaped her. The grass stung her, each tiny jolt of electricity a bit more painful than the last. Ignoring the pins and needles in her fingertips and toes from the fall, she pushed herself to her feet and ran out of the meadow as fast as she could. Her chest still hummed from the painful pulse of energy her mentor had thrown at her.

"Why do you insist on doing that?" she snapped.

"You need to get used to being hit. When you summon a sword or shield, you are exposing yourself as a host, and you should expect to be attacked. I'm merely preparing you."

"Gee, thanks," she said dryly.

"You're quite welcome."

She rolled her eyes, hands on her hips as she stared at him. Maybe he didn't understand sarcasm.

He nodded at her arm. "One of these days you'll be able to block those energy pulses with that shield. Until then, make sure you ice your muscles every night."

She groaned. This would hurt.

CHAPTER TWENTY

Hunched over a stack of crates outside Bertha's store, Audrey put her chin in her hands and blew a raspberry.

Bored.

She honestly felt a bit useless. She wished she knew magic. Hell, a part of her wished she had some kind of dark magic in her body, too. Even that was better than waiting in front of Bertha's shop for someone to buy a plit.

The stairs behind her creaked, and she knew without looking that Bertha had joined her outside. Sure enough, the shop's door clicked shut a second later.

"You're unhappy," Bertha said. It wasn't a question. It sounded more like an observation.

Audrey shrugged. "We came here to help Victoria, not me. I just wish I..."

When Audrey trailed off, Bertha gently nudged her shoulder. "What bothers you, little one?"

The answer was simple, yet impossible to put into words without immense guilt. Audrey wished she were special. God, it killed her to even admit that to herself, much less to Bertha.

For as long as she had known Victoria, Audrey had played second fiddle. She didn't mind for the most part, since it had been going on so long. Victoria was the gorgeous one and Audrey was the best friend. It had always been that way, and Victoria had always looked out for her. But since Audrey had come to Fairhaven, something had shifted within her. This place made her crave something more, something significant.

Bertha leaned on the crates as well, the wood straining from her weight as she set her elbows on the corners and watched the crowd pass. "I don't quite know what your friend Victoria is up to, and that's your business. But I can tell she's got something you wish you had. Can you at least tell me what that is?"

Audrey stared at her fingers, struggling to find the words. They had to be careful, even though Bertha had done so much for them. It still wasn't clear who they could trust with Victoria's secret, and Audrey wasn't about to expose her childhood friend for what she really was.

"She's training with Fyrn?" Bertha asked.

Audrey stiffened, but in hindsight it must have been obvious considering who they had asked for the night they met the ogre. She nodded.

"And for whatever reason, he didn't take you as his pupil as well," Bertha added.

Audrey hesitated. She knew the reason: she didn't have dark magic embedded in her forearm. Victoria would take more time to train, and thus she was his primary focus.

Understandable, if hard to swallow. Instead of clarifying, she nodded again.

Bertha gestured to her next-door neighbor. "Watch the shop for me, will you?"

The old ogre nodded.

"And you, little one, come with me," Bertha said with a stern look at Audrey over the bridge of her nose.

Audrey followed Bertha through the house, past the enchanted shelves filled with various meats and jars that somehow remained fresh despite a lack of refrigeration. Together, they lumbered through the kitchen and out into the backyard. For the first time since their arrival, Bertha opened the lock on the little shack in the back of the yard, standing outside and gesturing for Audrey to enter first.

Cautiously, Audrey ducked inside, scanning the walls without being sure what she would find.

Weapons. Holy shit, there were so many weapons.

The interior was far larger than it should have been, and the floor-to-ceiling mirrors on three of the walls reminded Audrey of her old dance studios. The fourth wall, which also held the door, was covered in every kind of weapon Audrey had ever seen in her life and then some. From swords to daggers to throwing stars, Bertha seemed to own at least one of everything. There was even a collection of oddly shaped blades the height of her body, with no hilts. In the center of it all were four wooden dummies, each riddled with scars from the blades and modeled after a different creature. Audrey recognized the ogre, wizard, and elf, but the last one was new.

Adrenalin shot through her as she wondered why Bertha had brought her in here, or why Bertha would even have access to such a place. She was a chef, a grocery store clerk, a small business owner. The lumbering ogre didn't strike Audrey as a fighter.

The floor creaked as Bertha entered and shut the door behind her. "This is my secret, Audrey. My joy. And should you want to share it with me, I will teach you what I know. You are a kind soul, little one, but I will teach you to be fierce as well. You can use these gifts for good, to help Victoria, if that's what you want. If not, at least you will be strong."

Bertha reached for a sword as long as Audrey's body and spun it, the blade moving so quickly that Audrey could see only blurs. Bertha embedded the blade in a tall wooden dummy in the middle of the floor. The resulting *thunk* echoed in the training space, sending a gleeful shiver down Audrey's back.

"Shall we begin?" Bertha quirked a giant eyebrow.

A broad grin stretched over Audrey's face. "Teach me everything."

Audrey practiced her swings in the bedroom she shared with Victoria late into the night, careful to move slowly so as not to slice the bedspreads or curtains. Bertha had begun to teach her the basics of wielding one of the smallest swords, as well as the difference between a powerful stance and one meant only to intimidate an opponent. It all came so easily, so effortlessly, that Audrey's spirits had been renewed. She had so impressed Bertha, in fact, that they were going to visit the ogre's brother tomorrow to talk about Audrey joining his Berserk team.

Perhaps Audrey wasn't living in Victoria's shadow after all.

The stairs creaked, far too quietly for it to be Bertha. Victoria must've come home. Audrey paused her practice, leaning the sword in one corner so she wouldn't maim whoever walked through the door. Sure enough, the door swung open a second later and smacked against the opposite wall. Victoria entered, eyes already drooping, long tears in her clothes. Quite a few burn marks had eaten significant chunks of her sleeves, and her hair was a frizzled mess. She collapsed on the bed, which Audrey was now paying for, and closed her eyes.

"Fun day?" Audrey said with a grin.

"Shut up," Victoria mumbled.

"Make any progress?"

Victoria nodded and sat upright, lifting her hands and staring at them. Her eyes narrowed a bit, and she clenched her hands into fists. A small shield appeared on her right hand, and a tiny dagger in her other palm. Audrey held her breath, waiting for them to disappear again, but they remained.

"It's something," Victoria said, the shield and dagger disappearing as she relaxed her grip on them.

"It's a lot better than something. You couldn't even come close to that this morning. You're learning fast."

Victoria nodded. "This is the hardest thing I've ever done, but it's worth it. I'm not going to stop until I master it."

"Good. That's why we're here, after all."

Victoria muttered something and laid back down.

"I have good news, too," Audrey said with a smile. "I'm learning to fight. Today I nearly decapitated a wooden practice dummy."

Victoria didn't reply. Her chest rose and fell in a rhythmic pattern, her head slightly off the mattress.

Wow, it must have been one hell of a day. Victoria never fell asleep that fast.

Proud of Victoria's progress, Audrey leaned against the wall. And yet despite her pride in Victoria's impressive improvement, she couldn't shake the intense surge of jealousy that hit her square in the chest. As always, Victoria had surpassed her. Despite the danger that came with partnering with a host, Audrey wanted to stand alongside Victoria, not watch from the sidelines like a soccer mom.

Oh, to be the special one, the one everyone fawned over. Just once.

With a heavy sigh, Audrey crawled into bed as well and blew out the candle on her bedside table. The warm light faded, replaced by the soft glow of the crystals overhead as it leaked through the windows. Audrey stared out into the night. Lights flickered through the windows of some of the homes down the alley behind Bertha's house, and Audrey wondered what their lives were like, these magical creatures who had lived their whole lives underground, hidden from the humans above. There was so much magic here, so much to discover.

So much to learn.

CHAPTER TWENTY-ONE

Fyrn sat in his office as the morning light filtered through his window, his hand stroking his beard as he studied the only book in his possession on the Rhazdon Artifacts. It had been banned centuries ago, most of the copies burned due to the in-depth nature of the material and the crown's tendency to bury dark magic under the rug as though it didn't exist. Fyrn rolled his eyes at the incompetence of the royals who ran Fairhaven, astonished they had ruled for so long.

If he wasn't careful they would sweep Victoria under the rug too, by killing her without a second thought.

Part of him didn't know why he bothered to help her, but deep down he couldn't lie to himself. This was his redemption. It was his chance to make things right where he had failed so long ago.

He shook his head to rid himself of that sentimental drivel. Time to focus.

Fyrn turned to the pages that listed the two hundred and three known artifacts, though he suspected many of the descriptions were flat-out wrong and many existing artifacts were missing entirely. Fear clouded people's judgment, which made the study of these sorts of things very difficult. If people like him were to have any success in protecting their cities and the magical world from these artifacts, they had to understand them.

Thus, he would continue his research right under the crown's nose.

Victoria had potential, certainly. She had already begun to control the weapons and the shield provided by the Rhazdon Artifact, though she was starting small. He had confidence she would improve very quickly, and with her increased skill would come arrogance. He would nip that in the bud every time he saw it. Worse, she was a quick learner hell-bent on revenge, which meant he ran the risk of her going after Luak before she was ready. Fyrn didn't know much about this Luak character, only the rumors that he had ingratiated himself with the royal inner circle, which was a bad sign. This elf was highly skilled in both magic and politics, which made him an adversary Victoria would not easily vanquish.

Which led him to an unfortunate question: what would help Victoria better handle her Rhazdon Artifact in a way that could help her take out such powerful adversary? So far, he only had one solution: another artifact.

The thought alone disgusted him. It was too risky, too foolhardy. He didn't even know what would happen to someone who had two artifacts. It was said this kind of dark magic could corrupt the very soul of whoever wielded it, but he had yet to study enough on the subject to know if that was fact or fiction. Perhaps corrupted souls were simply drawn to dark magic.

But was Victoria different?

Hmm. Perhaps he would need to observe her in a public setting over time. As her grasp of the Rhazdon Artifact improved, it might affect her demeanor. Part of her training would need to be done in crowds, around strangers. Fyrn would need to test her to see if her pure heart remained true as the Rhazdon Artifact further took hold.

He slammed the book shut and snapped his fingers. A floorboard sprang into the air and hovered, revealing a hidden safe beneath it. He set the book inside next to a few other select tomes that had been banned over the years.

Someone knocked on his door.

Victoria.

He crossed the living room and flung open the door. "You're late, V—"

Instead of the young blond woman he had begun to train, a familiar tall man in a wizard's cloak stood at the door. He wore long white robes with sapphires sewn into the hems and a golden pendant that hung nearly to his waist. A belt of blue silk tied his robe together, and he carried a tall black staff with a glimmering blue stone at the top.

Fyrn gritted his teeth, eyeing the unwanted guest. "Diesel."

"Fyrn," the young wizard smirked, peering over the threshold to scan the living room. His lip curled a bit in disgust.

"What do you—"

"Do you really live here, or is this more of an outhouse?"

"Go away. I don't have time for—"

"Of course you have time. After the trevor beetle incident in Washington D.C., I suspect you have all the time in the world."

Fyrn stiffened. He had hoped word wouldn't travel, but he knew that was too much to expect. No one ever really recovered from performing magic in front of humans, whether they were put to death or not. Only his decades of service had saved him from the guillotine, but the incident had ended his career. He had been stripped of his rank in the wizarding community and largely shunned ever since.

Fyrn frowned, not one to dwell on the past. "Have you come to gloat?"

"No, that's just a bonus. I came to ask about an incident that occurred in the gang district a few nights ago. Lots of loose cobblestones, gouges in the pavement, that kind of thing. It looked as though an all-out magical war took place in the street. Reports of flashes, white lights, wisps—"

"Your point?"

"My point is," Diesel said, narrowing his eyes, "that I'm part of the king's council, and he's tasked me with finding out what happened. The king doesn't take kindly to warfare in our streets, much less spells that suggest a witch or wizard was involved. Considering not many of us live in Fairhaven anymore, your name was mentioned as a possible suspect."

Uh oh.

In his best effort to appear calm, Fyrn waved away the thought. He wasn't good at lying, but Diesel's head was too far up his own ass to notice. "I'm too busy studying to involve myself with nonsense."

"Studying what, exactly?"

"How to turn pompous wizards into shoots of bamboo, actually," Fyrn snapped. "Now get out."

Diesel set his foot against the door, blocking it as Fyrn tried to slam it in his face. "If you're implicated, Fyrn, there will be consequences. You were great once, but you've lost your touch. No one will vouch for you."

"The same will someday happen to you."

"I doubt it. The people and their king all love me," Diesel said with an arrogant grin on his face.

"For now. That will change."

"If only—"

"Is everything okay?" a woman asked.

Diesel jumped, tilting his staff in the subtle attack position all wizards were trained to use when caught off-guard. Victoria stood behind him, hands on her hips, mercifully wearing a long-sleeved shirt that hid her Rhazdon Artifact. The pixie hummed alongside her, the metal in his wings glistening as it reflected the crystalline daylight.

Adrenaline pumped through Fyrn, making him dizzy, but he did his best to hide it. He hadn't heard her approach, and apparently neither had Diesel. She was already getting so much better, and the Rhazdon Artifact in her arm seemed to give her additional gifts. It set her apart, and right now that could get her killed.

Diesel flashed her a charming smile, one Fyrn had often seen directed at the young women who admired and fawned over him at events in the palace. "Hello, there. I'm Diesel Armstrong. What's your name?"

An expression crossed her face that Fyrn hadn't seen before—a combination of entertainment and wariness. "Victoria Brie."

"Like the—"

"Yes, the cheese," she said, rolling her eyes.

"An honor." Diesel lifted her right hand and kissed her knuckles.

In unison, Victoria and Fyrn tensed. It seemed she was as worried as he was that her sleeve would slide up, but the fabric stayed in place.

"Charmed," she said dryly.

Diesel stood a bit taller, puffing out his chest like a man flexing to impress women on a beach. "I must confess, you're not supposed to follow me when I'm on official duty, but I'm honored nonetheless that a beauty such as yourself would seek me out. Is there a question I can answer for you?"

Victoria hesitated. "What?"

Diesel gestured to the house. "Surely you're not here for the scenery."

Victoria caught Fyrn's eye, grimacing slightly as she silently asked for clarification. Fyrn groaned, rubbing his face in annoyance. "Diesel, she's here to see me."

Diesel laughed, a charming and melodic sound that would have wooed any regular woman. But Victoria was far from normal, and Fyrn was grateful she wouldn't fall for his nonsense.

"It's true," she said.

Diesel hesitated, smile faltering. "Why would you waste your time on his low-level tricks? I can show you far more than this charlatan."

"Charlatan?" She bristled, balling her hands into fists.

"Enough, Victoria."

"But Fyrn—"

"Enough. Good day, Diesel."

Diesel shook his head, still laughing, and proceeded down the trail away from the cottage. He shot one last dashing grin over his shoulder. "Suit yourself, sweet Victoria, but should you ever want a true mentor, you can find me at the palace."

Instead of watching Diesel retreat toward the road, Victoria glared at Fyrn with barely contained fury. "How could you let him talk to you like that?"

"Diesel is a nuisance, nothing more. He is gifted enough with magic to have caught the king's attention, but what he thinks doesn't matter. Public opinion, playing to what people think of you—it's all worthless. All that matters is what you know, and I know more than any of them."

"Fyrn, public perception is important. When I first got here, people laughed when I said I was looking for you."

He shrugged. "It doesn't bother me. None of them can do what I can."

"But if they knew—"

"It's time to get to work." He pushed past her and led the way toward the tunnel they had taken yesterday. Today would be another challenging one for Victoria, and he needed her to focus. It didn't matter that fools like Diesel had no respect for him. When the time came Fyrn would prove his worth once more to the person who mattered most: himself.

"What's the purpose of this game again?" Audrey leaned into Bertha, her voice low to keep anyone on the field from hearing.

They sat in the first row of empty bleachers lining a small field on the outskirts of Fairhaven. Bertha had closed her shop for the afternoon to introduce Audrey to the game of Berserk.

And dear God, did it earn that name.

On the field, ogres and elves faced off in mixed teams. They charged each other round after round, the yells like battle cries as they rammed into each other. Limbs broke. Helmets flew into the stands. Ogres were flipped onto their backs, the ground shaking from the force. And there was lots and *lots* of cursing.

Audrey loved every second of it. She did not, however, understand the rules at all.

"You see those colorful little creatures down there?" Bertha pointed to what looked like a net filled with gold, green, and black spheres lying on the moss nearby.

"Those are creatures? They look like balls."

"They're called fidgets and are very much alive. Look closer."

Audrey watched the net closely, only to realize the fuzzy spheres inside were squirming. Every now and then a bit of furry skin would lift and a set of eyes would peek through, darting around for a second before disappearing once more.

"Whoa," Audrey said, leaning back.

"Fidgets are notoriously difficult to catch. They skitter over the ground, racing in every direction, but they're kept on the field by these barriers." Bertha tapped the short wooden fence separating the bleachers from the field. Its planks were so close together there was no hope of a fidget ever squirming through the gaps.

"So the players have to catch them?"

Bertha nodded. "The gold are worth ten points, the black fifty, and the green are worth a hundred. When you catch one, you take it over to one of those three bins on the opponent's side."

On each end, three silver bins were spaced across the full width of the field. "Doesn't that hurt the…what did you call them? Fidgets?"

Bertha chuckled. "Nothing can hurt a fidget. They're indestructible, and they love to run. They seem to enjoy this as much as we do, since it's basically a game of chase for them."

Audrey chuckled. "Funny, it's a little like Quidditch. More blood, though."

Bertha quirked a giant eyebrow. "It's like what, now?"

Audrey faltered. She should have known better than to drop a pop culture reference on an ogre. "It's, uh, a game from a fantasy story about witches and wizards."

"So… real life?"

Audrey chuckled as she surveyed the magical city around them filled with creatures she had only dreamed could exist. "Yeah, I guess so."

While grunts of pain and victory rolled over the playing field, Audrey studied the net filled with fidgets as a gold one stared at the melee. It squeaked and inched toward the grass as though it wanted to join the elves and ogres as they flattened each other.

She shook her head. This place was so weird, but she loved it anyway.

On the field, an ogre flipped an elf onto his back, the elf's forearm snapping as it hit the ground. He yelled in agony, and Audrey grimaced. Quidditch was fun, but Berserk was way more brutal. "If it's just a game of catch-the-critter, why are they attacking each other like that?"

"Never you fret, little one—we have a wizard medic who makes everyone right as rain after the match. You're out of the game as soon as you go to him, though, so be smart about when you choose to get healed. This means that as the game progresses, there are fewer and fewer players to protect each other and the bins. The fewer players you have on your team, the less chance you have of winning. It's your duty to your team to soldier on unless you're about to die."

"Uh huh," Audrey said weakly.

Bertha pointed to the ogres and elves running around the field before them. "There are ten men—or women, in your case—on each team, and each has a purpose. You have the fidget finders, who chase after the fidgets, obviously. Usually, those are the smallest and fastest members, and we have only one or two on a team. Aside from the fidget finders, you have the keep. Now, the keep stays by the goal, and his duty is to tackle anyone from the opposite team who dares try to score. The third position on the team is the runners. They, well—"

Two ogres interrupted Bertha as they smashed into each other nearby, growling as if they were at war. They grappled for several seconds, each trying to overtake the other. Bones snapped, and one ogre finally fell to the ground, nursing his shoulder. The victor roared into the sky and ran off to find someone else to mutilate.

Audrey gulped. "I take it those are runners?"

Bertha chuckled. "Indeed. And that, dear one, is what makes Berserk the prized sport of Fairhaven. Being on a proper Berserk team is a path to fame and glory down here. The only rule is no magic, and everything else is fair play."

"You actually want me to go on that field? Strategically, won't all those massive ogres just try to flatten me at once?"

"That's a solid strategy, yes."

Audrey frowned at Bertha's indifference. "Awesome."

"But that's why we have our runners, little one! They'll intercept anyone who tries to take you out. Usually."

Audrey leaned against the barrier around the field, suddenly doubting how much she wanted to play this game. Something about trusting strangers to keep her from being crushed beneath a giant ogre didn't sit well with her.

Bertha pointed again at the net of indestructible creatures nearby. "When you catch one of the fidgets, the opposing team will try to steal it. To protect you, a runner on your team will likely come to take it from you so you can focus on finding another. There are four rounds, fifteen minutes each. Get the most points by the last buzzer, and your team wins. It's fairly simple."

An ogre roared at centerfield, digging his claws into another ogre's side as they faced off. Audrey gulped. "Yeah, simple."

Bertha nodded. "You'll fit right in."

"Are you, uh, trying to kill me? Serious question."

The shopkeeper laughed so hard she held her sides. "Always the funny one, you are. You will catch the fidgets, little one. That's all. The others will protect you."

"Time!" one of the ogres shouted. The team members skidded to a halt, some patting each other on the back while others limped toward the healing wizard, who sat and read a book at the opposite end of the bleachers.

The ogre who had called time jogged over to Audrey and Bertha, smiling despite the bruises on his face from practice. Bertha stood and hugged him over the wooden fence separating the field from the seats. "Edgar, you've gotten fat!"

"You and your compliments," he said with a chuckle.

Audrey laughed weakly. Ogres, man. Freaking ogres.

"Is this the recruit?" Edgar asked, nodding to Audrey.

"She is. Quite the quick learner. I think she has some Oriceran blood in her," Bertha said with a wink.

"Let's see what you can do, little one," he said, extending a hand.

Audrey took it, and he flung her over the barrier in what must have been an attempt to simply help her over it. She stumbled a bit as she found her footing on the other side, but thankfully she didn't eat dirt during her first meeting with the team.

"Sorry! You're light as a pillow," he said.

Audrey shrugged. "It's okay. What do I need to do?"

He lifted the net filled with fidgets. "Catch as many of these as you can before I call time. Ready?"

"Do you have any advice on how to—"

"Go!" He pulled open the drawstring on the net and tossed it a good twenty feet toward centerfield. The fidgets jumped out and tore off in a dozen directions, fast as cats running from a bathtub of water.

Audrey bolted toward the nearest one, a gold fidget. It zigzagged. Careful and focused, she tensed, preparing to pounce. It bolted left.

Patience.

It bolted right.

Hold on, almost there.

It bolted left again.

Now!

She jumped, putting her full weight on the fidget as she trapped it beneath her body. It squirmed, its skin surprisingly like the slick body of a dolphin, but she kept it in place. She lifted it over her head like a trophy. A pair of eyes peeked at her through a gap in the creature's round body, and its tiny pink tongue blew a raspberry at her.

Bertha clapped, and Edgar whistled from the sidelines. "Good! Eleven more to go!"

Audrey grinned. This was actually kind of awesome.

Completely and utterly focused on the moment, Victoria lifted her arms and summoned the largest shield she could hold continuously. It protected her head and most of her chest, but she needed both hands to hold it. It overburdened her like a barbell carrying just a bit too much weight. She gritted her teeth, straining every muscle in her body to keep it upright.

The static charge of another of Fyrn's attacks crackled

through the air, and she braced herself for impact. She needed to learn how to take a hit, but God did it hurt.

Sure enough, the bolt crashed into her shield, knocking her backward. She slid across the ground, rocks scratching her back as she bounced over the rough floor. She cursed as she rolled the last few feet.

Ow.

Battered and bruised, Victoria struggled to stand. Her arms and legs shook, weak from having done this for hours already. Down here in their little training cave, she had no idea what time it was or how long they had been here, but she tried not think about it. All that mattered was learning to control the Rhazdon Artifact's powers, and she would stay for as long as it took.

Above her, Styx chuckled softly. For whatever reason, he got a kick out of it every time she tumbled head over heels into the shock grass.

"Tiny little traitor," she said, shaking her head.

"Good job, Victoria," Fyrn said with a nod, tapping his staff twice on the rocky ground. It seemed to be his version of applause—at least the closest thing to it she would ever get from him.

"Again," she said, bracing herself.

"It's important to rest, Victoria."

She dug her heel into the rocky floor, eyes focused on him as she prepared for another attack. "Again!"

Audrey jogged to where Bertha and Edgar waited on the

sidelines, shoulders heaving as she caught her breath. "How'd I do?"

Edgar blinked rapidly, his mouth gaping. "How... how did you..."

Bertha laughed, the hearty sound carrying across the field. "I told you she would be a good fit!"

"All twelve! You caught all of them! That's impossible. You even caught the green ones!"

Audrey grinned. Those had been tough at first until she realized the gold irises of their eyes peeking through the grass gave them away. After that, it was cake.

"You're just a small human! How did you catch all twelve of those fidgets?"

She shrugged. "You said I had to."

Edgar chuckled. "Astounding. Yes, obviously you're on my team. Don't dream of going to another one, do you hear? I'll never win again if you do. If you have a twin, we need one more fidget finder."

Audrey beamed, grateful for the compliment and certain Victoria would love this game. "What's our team's name? The Snarxes? The Trevor Beetles? What's our mascot?"

"The Plits!" Bertha clapped her hands together, laughing almost too hard to speak.

Audrey hesitated, glancing between the ogre siblings as she tried to figure out if it was a joke. "Like the fruit?"

Edgar rolled his eyes. "I lost a bet."

With a chuckle, Audrey shrugged. "The Plits it is."

CHAPTER TWENTY-TWO

Back from her afternoon at the playing field, Audrey effortlessly sliced a melon in half with her new sword, a congratulations gift from Bertha. She smiled, pleased with her progress in weapons training. She had started to turn her chores into training exercises, and it was paying off.

She wiped the blade on her pants and laid the sword on the table. Gathering the melon slices in her hands, she poured them onto the paper wrapper Bertha had laid out for the customer waiting outside the shop. A few folds later, Audrey hefted the heavy packages of sliced melon in her hands and walked outside.

A regal elf in an ornate red gown stood with her hands folded in front of her, a warm smile on her lips as Bertha spoke about a recent trip to another city.

"It was a beautiful kemana, but not nearly as wonderful as our Fairhaven," Bertha said with a wink.

"Not much can compete with our fair home," the elf said, her voice as lovely as her face.

Audrey smiled and offered the wrapped melon. "Here you go."

"Thank you, sweet soul," the elf said, taking the package.

"Until next time, Merida," Bertha said with a wave.

"Farewell," Merida said, joining the crowd. She stood out like a sore thumb, a stunning crimson beacon in a sea of green, gray, and brown.

"Who is she?" Audrey asked.

"An old friend from my home kemana."

"Where's that?"

Bertha's shoulders drooped, and she sighed wistfully. "That's a story for another time, but I can say I'll never return. It was overrun, and the ogres were forced to flee. Elves like Merida ensured we could travel safely."

"Whoa, heavy. What happened?" Audrey tentatively patted Bertha's shoulder, but the ability to comfort others didn't come naturally.

"We'll discuss it another day, little one. For now, be grateful for what we have here. Kemanas like Fairhaven are coveted by the powerful. There are those who want what we have, who want to control the city and those who live in it."

Audrey watched the crowd as strangers passed, still too many types of creatures to name even though she was getting used to it here. It had never occurred to her that there might be unrest here, or occupation and war. It was such a beautiful, peaceful place.

"Are you okay, Bertha?"

The ogre nodded, smiling. "Thank you. I'm fine. You take your break. I'll watch the front of the store for a bit."

"Okay, I will..." Audrey lost her train of thought as a familiar face bobbed through the crowd, and it took her a second to recognize him as the thief Victoria had tackled not long ago. His shifty eyes scanned the crowd and settled on something she couldn't see. Quick as lightning, he snatched a pouch off a goblin's waist, fingers apparently light enough that the goblin didn't even notice. The thief darted through the crowd and slid down an alley.

"I'll be right back, Bertha," Audrey said. Before the ogre could protest, Audrey ran into the crowd, chasing him as fast as she could without bumping into anyone on her way. She entered the alley he had taken, a dark place with no foot traffic, just as he turned down another alley not far off.

Careful to measure her breathing and keep her pace steady, she raced after him, slowing only to carefully look around each corner before she followed. She was gaining on him, only about twenty feet off now, when he paused and jogged up some stairs onto a back porch.

She slowed, keeping to the building's wall as she neared.

"...and the girl?" a familiar voice asked.

Dread shot clear to her toes as she recognized the voice, and Audrey stopped dead in her tracks. Before she could help herself, fear hit her like a cold wave as she relived her last run-in with the elf she had shot in the bank parking lot.

Luak.

"Her name is Victoria Brie. The friend is Audrey, but I haven't figured out her last name."

"Where do they go?"

"Mainly the ogre's shop. Victoria goes off in the mornings, but I can't keep up with her."

"And the incident in the gang district?"

"Yeah, it was definitely her. I saw her myself. She's a host. I knew she was unnatural."

"Tell no one."

"But—"

"No one."

"Yes, sir."

The familiar clink of crystals reminded Audrey of all the times customers had handed over a small collection of them to pay for the week's groceries. It seemed the thief was being well compensated for his information.

"What are you going to do with them?" the thief asked.

Around the corner and thankfully out of sight, Luak chuckled darkly. "They'll get what they deserve."

Audrey tensed. As much as she wanted to kill this guy, she couldn't face Luak alone, armed with only her sword and a couple days' training. Footsteps thudded on the stoop, and she pressed herself as close to the alley wall as she could to hide as they left.

The footsteps faded, but she waited a good five minutes before she headed back to the shop.

Luak had found them. She had to warn Victoria.

Back at home, Audrey aimlessly polished her sword's blade as she replayed the day in her mind. What a rollercoaster.

The door swung open and smacked against the wall.

Audrey jumped, caught off-guard. Victoria ambled in like a zombie and crashed face-first on the bed.

"Hello there, buttercup," Audrey said dryly.

"My everything hurts," Victoria mumbled through the comforter.

"You didn't think revenge would be a cakewalk, did you?"

Vitoria pushed herself upright and leaned against the headboard. "Thanks for the sympathy."

Audrey blew her a kiss and set her sword aside.

"What's that for?" Victoria nodded toward the blade.

"Bertha's training me to fight."

Victoria quirked an eyebrow. "Bertha can fight?"

"I know, right? And she's really good."

"That's awesome. Are you enjoying it?"

Audrey nodded, smile wide as she relived her first day in the training room. "I swear she has every weapon in existence. It's like walking into a museum of death."

Victoria grinned. "Sweet."

"Bertha also introduced me to a game they play here called Berserk. It's really fun. She got me onto a team and everything. Since we don't have our kickboxing classes anymore, I think you should join."

"Ha, right. Fyrn would love that."

"Who knows? Maybe you could spin it as a training exercise. You're clever."

Victoria chuckled. "If you say it's fun, I'll give it a try. What do you do?"

"Catch little round creatures that look like balls while ogres and elves tackle each other around you."

In the stunned silence that followed, Victoria grimaced a bit and stared at Audrey. "This place is so weird."

"I know. It's awesome."

Victoria yawned deeply, stretching her arms as she fell back onto the bed. "I'm beat. I think I'll hit the hay."

Audrey's smile faded. She didn't really want to share the news about Luak, but Victoria would fall asleep any second, and this couldn't wait another day. "Wait, I have to tell you something first. It's bad. Really bad."

Victoria sat up, her eyelids drooping. "What is it?"

"Luak found us. He knows you're here, and they're watching Bertha's place."

"Shit." Victoria rubbed her eyes.

"Pretty much. What do we do?"

Victoria's jaw tightened, and she stared out the window for several minutes without saying a word. Audrey waited, not wanting to interrupt the train of thought puffing down the tracks in Victoria's brain.

"We wait," Victoria finally said.

"Are you crazy? He knows where we live! Again!"

She gritted her teeth. "I know, okay? I know. Don't you think I want to hunt him down more than anything? But let's be real—he knows where we are, and we have no idea where *he* is except that he's close. He must have followed us, which means he can do it again. Our next move should be strategic, and running out of here in the middle of the night would raise flags. I'm not ready to face him yet, and he hasn't done anything here I can nail him for. He's likely planning an attack, so we'll plan our own. We got lucky with this info, but let's not rely on luck anymore. Deal?"

"Deal."

"I'll talk to Fyrn in the morning and see if he has more ideas. For now, get some rest."

"If you say so, boss."

Victoria smirked and threw a pillow at her. Audrey deflected it and sat back on her bed, staring at the dimly glowing crystals that served as her stars.

Wait for the murderer to plan his attack. What could possibly go wrong?

"You want to do *what*?"

Victoria cleared her throat and jogged to catch up with Fyrn as he entered the tunnel that would take them to the training cave. "I want to play Berserk. It sounds fun."

"You have a painfully skewed idea of what constitutes 'fun.'"

"C'mon, you know I'm much better already. I can control the sword and shield. I don't summon them anymore when startled. It would be good to practice in a public setting so I can get used to being around people again."

"I see right through you. You're trying to sell me on this."

She blew a raspberry. "Look, I could just go play without permission, Grandpa Grump. I asked first not to get your blessing but to get your honest opinion. Do you think I'm ready to be around people?"

He hummed a bit to himself, stroking his beard as his staff tapped the rocky ground with every step. "I think you are, yes."

She grinned, grateful she hadn't overestimated her progress thus far. She jogged ahead, even more excited for today's sparring.

Victoria huffed, chasing after a little golden fidget as it careened across the field. Eyes on her prize, she dove for it and grabbed the little critter in her hands. Hoisting it over her head, she grinned triumphantly. Bertha and Audrey cheered on the sidelines.

"That's your third fidget in five minutes!" Edgar shouted, hands on his head in apparent disbelief.

She bowed. "Shall I keep going?"

"No, I've seen enough. You two are definitely on my team. Who knew humans were so talented?"

In unison, Victoria and Audrey snorted in annoyance.

Ogres.

CHAPTER TWENTY-THREE

In the dark and twisting tunnels beneath Fairhaven, Victoria followed Fyrn's lead as he lit the way back to the city. Weeks had passed, and she grew stronger every day. She trained with Fyrn during the day and played Berserk with her fellow Plits at night.

She shook her head at their stupid team name, but she loved those jocks anyway.

Styx sat on her shoulder, humming to himself as he kicked his legs and enjoyed the free ride. Victoria, however, wasn't enjoying herself quite as much. She stared at the back of Fyrn's head, debating how to word what she considered to be a very important question, the answer to which she didn't think she would like.

"Why are you staring at me?" he asked without turning around.

Freaky. It was like this guy had eyes in the back of his head. "You're not going to like it."

"I'm sure I've encountered worse."

So be it, then. "What did my parents catch you doing? You said they badgered you, but I know them. They would only have done that if you deserved it. What did you do?"

He sighed, stopping in his tracks and resting his full weight against his staff. "I suspect you'll hear about it eventually."

"Tell me. Please." She waited, arms crossed as she studied him. He moved slowly, as if he had suddenly donned a great weight, but he never once turned around.

"Various governments in the human world used to recruit me occasionally to take care of magical creatures and the odd rogue wizard who made it their way. Most of the human world knows nothing about Fairhaven or magic, and the Order of the Silver Griffins prefers it that way. But some, those in power, have just enough of the knowledge to protect the humans from the true dangers magic can bring."

"And you helped them?"

He nodded, looking just a bit over his shoulder at her. "I was called to your capital in D.C. to exterminate a swarm of trevor beetles that had nested under the Capitol building. They're attracted to lies, after all. They're nasty, flesh-eating bugs that travel in swarms and eat people alive. If I didn't do something, hundreds would die bite by bite, alive and screaming the whole time."

Victoria whistled. "Wow, that bad?"

Fyrn nodded. "This nest was massive, easily a hundred or more, and something had to be done. I was called in, but about a dozen escaped. They made it to the surface and caused enough trouble that it was deemed a terrorist attack. Biological warfare."

"Yikes."

"Yikes, indeed. It was horrible. In the end, forty people died and hundreds were injured. To stop the creatures from killing anymore innocent people, I had to perform magic in front of humans. That's punishable by death."

She sucked in a sharp breath. "How did you—"

He silenced her with a wave of his hand. "I erased their memories and made them think it was terrorism—the alternative was to expose mankind to magic, and that would be far worse. Because of my experience, my history in the kemanas, and my knowledge of magic, I was granted a one-time pardon but was stripped of both my rank and title. I survived, sure, but the guilt weighs on me. I have never in my life failed so completely at any task. And your parents…" He gritted his teeth, grip tightening on his staff.

"What?" she asked softly, almost afraid of the answer.

"They filmed the entire ordeal. There, on camera, was irrefutable evidence of magic. They threatened to expose me if I didn't tell them what they wanted to know. I tried to erase their memories and destroy the tape, but they made copies. I couldn't find all of the evidence, and they set up failsafes to expose me if something happened to them. My hands were tied."

Heart heavy with the guilt of what her parents had done, Victoria couldn't look him in eye. She studied the ground as if it were interesting, ashamed of her parents' choice even while understanding that as journalists they often felt they didn't have the luxury to choose. They did what they needed to do to expose the truth, even if it meant putting themselves in harm's way or making demands that others felt were unreasonable.

"They never would have actually done it," she said softly.

He shrugged. "I know that now, and that's why I dismissed them in the end. For a time there, however, I told them far more than I should have. I felt as though I was without a choice. You can understand why I wasn't excited to see you."

She nodded. "I'm sorry."

He shook his head. "Water under the—"

"No," she interrupted. "I'm sorry for what they did. It was wrong. I loved them dearly, and I miss them with all my heart, but I can admit when something is wrong. They strong-armed you, and that was not fair, especially considering that the act they were blackmailing you for was so—"

"Shameful," he said softly, his grip tightening on his staff.

A knot formed in Victoria's throat, and she ran her thumb over the Rhazdon Artifact in her arm to distract herself. "Did you help my dad get this?"

Fyrn shook his head. "I don't know where he got it, and most of me doesn't want to find out."

Fyrn resumed their trek back to Fairhaven, and for a moment Victoria stayed put and watched him walk away. Styx flitted overhead and settled into her hair, chattering softly.

He was shaking.

"Hush, you're okay," she said, running a finger over his back to help calm him. For the first time, that technique didn't help at all. He trembled harder, staring at something over her shoulder.

She followed his gaze, a flicker of anxiety igniting in her chest. The hair on the back of her neck stood on end, and the sensation of being watched grew stronger with every second that passed.

In the shadows, deep within the tunnel they had just walked down, something slithered.

"I saw it too," Shiloh said, suddenly beside her.

She cursed and jumped a good foot in the air, hand on her heart as she pressed herself against the rock wall. "For Christ's sake, stop doing that!"

"No. I'm starting to enjoy your reaction," he said, examining his cuticles. Faster than she could complain, he disappeared.

That damn ghost.

The adrenaline fading, she once again surveyed the dark tunnel. Ears straining for any sign of the slithering entity, she heard only the steady drip of water hitting the floor somewhere close by. Her body lit up with nerves, and she didn't fully understand why. Whatever it was, whatever had just passed, she knew in her gut it was bad news.

"Victoria, let's go," Fyrn said sharply, his voice echoing a bit.

She jogged over to him. "I saw something slither by."

"Not surprising. That's why you need to stay close. Lots of things live down here. These monsters keep everyone else away, which makes this a prime place for you to train safely." He continued walking down the tunnel toward his cabin, and Victoria spent most of the trek looking over her shoulder.

The dread that clung to her didn't make sense. She

didn't care what Fyrn said; whatever that thing had been, it was more than just another animal living in the tunnels. Every fiber of her being told her that she never, ever wanted to see it again.

Victoria sat on her bed, staring at the ceiling as night fell outside. She couldn't shake the image of the slithering tail, and the more she thought about it, the more she panicked. She did her best to alleviate the anxiety with lots of deep breaths, but it only got worse.

"Chill the hell out," Audrey said from her spot by the window. "You're starting to freak me out, and I don't even know what you're upset about."

Victoria rubbed her face. "I was trying to be subtle. Is it that bad?"

Audrey laughed. "You only sigh this much when something's wrong. You're as transparent as glass."

Victoria blew a raspberry. "I saw something in the tunnels. Something bad."

Audrey sat on Victoria's bed, frowning. "What was it?"

Victoria shook her head. "That's the problem. I'm not sure yet."

"What if—"

The stairs creaked heavily, sighing and cracking under the weight of someone rather large. Bertha, probably.

Sure enough, a few seconds later Bertha opened the door with a smile and a handful of crystals. "Audrey, you've been doing so well that I wanted to give you a little something so you two could buy yourselves something nice. It's good to treat yourself to the finer things on occasion."

Victoria smiled. "Thank you, Bertha."

"You're very kind," Audrey said, giving her mentor a hug as she retrieved the denni. Victoria grabbed the pouch her parents had given her out of Audrey's bag and set it on the bed. She untied the string and opened it for Audrey to slide them inside, exposing the contents to Bertha in the process.

Before Audrey could add the new crystals, the ogre seemed to choke, eyes wide as she stared at the bag. "Good heavens, little humans, why are you working for me?"

Victoria's gaze shifted between the ogre and the money. "Is it a lot?"

"I—is it—yes!"

"Oh, sorry. We didn't know," Audrey set Bertha's payment back in her massive hand.

"Why are you running around with that much money in a backpack?" Bertha snapped.

"Bertha, we don't understand the value of your currency yet," Victoria said.

Audrey shrugged. "I've been starting to get a feel for what prices are on food, but that's about it. Think about it. We haven't even bought our own clothes yet. We're still wearing what your friend made us. We didn't know how far this bag would take us in terms of housing, clothing, and everything else we need. We also didn't know how long you would let us stay here. Besides, what is there, a bank we could put this in?"

"Yes!" Bertha shouted.

"Oh," Victoria and Audrey said in unison.

Bertha set the money in Audrey's palm and clicked her tongue in disapproval when she tried to protest. The great big ogre lifted a massive finger and waved it in her face. "First thing tomorrow, we're going to the bank. I'll teach you how to be proper citizens of Fairhaven yet!"

Victoria wouldn't make her training with Fyrn today. She had tried to sneak out in the morning, but Bertha had awakened early, likely to stop Victoria from bailing on the bank visit. No amount of protest had worked on the ogre, who said she would lose her mind if all that denni remained upstairs in her guest room. It apparently made them a target for bandits or even murderers, and Bertha wasn't having it. To top it all off, she demanded they buy a proper wardrobe and—gag—a gown or two while they were out. Out of respect for her host, Victoria obeyed. At least Bertha had sent a cryptic message via a mail clerk to let Fyrn know Victoria would be unavailable, so he wouldn't wonder.

Skipping practice to bank and shop. Fyrn wouldn't like it, but Victoria had to admit that a moment or two of relaxation sounded nice.

Bertha led the way through Fairhaven's streets, Victoria and Audrey in tow. This was a section of town they hadn't seen before, filled with ornate red and black buildings that towered far overhead. The bricks pulsated with a pale glow, and immense stained-glass windows let in light.

"Ah, this is it," Bertha said, gesturing to a tall silver building. "The only bank worth using."

They entered to find a massive main hall with a central crystal chandelier as large as an RV. Aside from the three of them, there was no one in the building.

"I guess others don't find it as wonderful as you," Audrey said.

Bertha lightly smacked Audrey on the back of the head. "Hush. There are magical protections in place so that no one knows who enters and who leaves. It allows you to protect your valuables and wealth."

Victoria grinned. "Nifty."

Two footprints glowed on the floor. Underneath, a row of symbols kept changing, fading in and out until finally they said, "Stand here."

"Which of you has the pouch?" Bertha asked.

"Me," Victoria said with a gentle wave of her hand, the pouch in her palm.

"You first, then," Bertha said.

Victoria set her feet on the moss-green footprints, her size-eight shoes dwarfed by the massive outline that told her where to stand. She waited, expecting something to happen, but nothing did. Confused, she peeked over her shoulder to ask Bertha what else to do.

No one was there.

In the blink of an eye, the brilliant white foyer faded to black. One by one, pinpricks of green light appeared in the darkness, surrounding her until a gentle light revealed that she was now in a small room, perhaps ten feet by ten feet at the most. She bit back her panic, not altogether happy with the idea of being transported somewhere without her knowledge or permission, but she gritted her teeth and stood a little taller to make herself feel braver.

A glowing handprint appeared in front of her, easily four times the size of hers.

"Verify your identity," a woman's voice said. It was as beautiful and melodic as a song, and Victoria was momentarily mesmerized by the mere sound of it.

It took a moment for her to regain her composure. "How?"

"Set your palm against the handprint," the voice said.

Well, Victoria was already in it this far. She might as well go all in. With a shrug, she obeyed.

"Hmmm," the voice said.

The handprint disappeared. Behind the wall, several gears clunked and ground against each other. The heavy rush of wood sliding over metal, muffled by the wall, suggested something would burst through any minute. Victoria waited, not altogether certain she would like whatever happened next.

Where the handprint had been, a silver door appeared. It slid open, and a wooden treasure chest came through. It rotated, as if handled by invisible hands, and the top popped open.

The chest was filled to the brim with crystals. Large and small, there were more than she could count. If Bertha thought the pouch had been full of riches, she would probably lose her shit just from looking at this trunk.

"I think this must be a mistake," Victoria said to the mysterious woman helping her.

"You are listed as an accessor of the account for Michael and Alison Brie. Do you know these humans?"

"Yes," she said softly, staring at the chest in bewilderment.

"Then there is no mistake. You have four more chests available to you. Would you like to see them?"

"Fuck, yes," she said, grinning.

More muffled clinks and whirs bled through the wall. Victoria waited, her smile broadening with every second. Sure enough, the four chests slid out of the wall and opened for her. Aside from a blank journal, a diamond amulet, and two more empty pouches, every chest was filled with crystals.

Victoria set her hands on her head, speechless as she stared at the chests. *Holy shit.* Rich in both worlds.

She emptied about half of what she had brought with her into one of the chests, but her smile began to fade as the crystals clinked against each other. Her parents had hidden so much. They had lied to her, blackmailed wizards, and lived secret lives.

Did she really know them?

A knot formed again in her throat, and she didn't try to push it back. She desperately wanted to cry. Grief would be welcome at this point, but every time she tried the delve into her sorrow, her fearsome anger bubbled forth instead. She grimaced at the surge of hatred for Luak, glaring at the nearest chest without even seeing it.

Her mother and father had always cared for her and loved her. Whatever mistakes they had made in life, they had not deserved to die the way they did.

She grabbed her much lighter pouch and tucked the diamond amulet inside. With her anger fresh and hot once more, she was determined not to spend the entire day shopping. This afternoon she would once more stand in the training cave so that she could continue to learn to defeat Luak. The elvish bastard would pay with his life for what he had done to her, and now Victoria had the riches of a small country to help her beat him.

He didn't stand a chance.

CHAPTER TWENTY-FOUR

I t only took twelve hours to buy a new house.

Alone in the massive dwelling, Audrey threw a jab at a handmade punching bag in the basement gym. She now shared a four-story townhouse with Victoria in what Bertha assured them was Fairhaven's safest district. She couldn't lie—she had been impressed that they were able to close on a house so quickly. It helped that Bertha seemed to know everyone and had a few favors to cash in, and it probably hadn't hurt that Victoria now had the wealth of an oil baron. Jingling crystals had exchanged hands, and before much time had passed she and Victoria had been given keys.

Audrey paused, wiping the sweat from her forehead as she took a quick break. At least her bestie was sharing the wealth.

The first game of the Berserk season was coming up, so Edgar had helped her set up the makeshift gym in the basement. They would add more equipment soon. In fact, the entire Berserk team might come over and do their weight training here if she decked it out enough, and the thought made her happy. It didn't offer much in the way of natural lighting, though, so she would need to find some gas lamps or candles for her nighttime workouts. For now, thin rays of light poured through the small windows that ran along the walls close to the ceiling. There wasn't much in the house yet, and even her little punching bag had been hand-made with some sawdust and a feed satchel she had borrowed from Bertha. But now that she didn't have to work, she needed to occupy herself somehow.

Thus, she would practice until she couldn't hold her arms up anymore.

A bit of her energy back now, Audrey threw a cross, and her homemade punching bag sailed backward on the metal chain that suspended it from a support beam. She coiled her body as she launched a roundhouse kick, and her ankle smacked against the bag, knocking it backward once again.

Bertha had promised more sword training later, and if Audrey learned that skill, they would also practice with daggers. Hell, maybe she should leave early and help Bertha with the store, just for old time's sake. She actually missed it a little.

She threw a combo at the bag, frowning as she focused all her strength, attention, and—if she were being honest with herself—jealousy into every blow.

A blast of green light assaulted Victoria, and it took every-thing in her, every ounce of focus, to maintain her massive shield. She gritted her teeth, straining every muscle in her body to hold the shield up, but it was so damn heavy.

She and Fyrn fought once more in the training tunnel, and every day they visited, she improved in spades. She could now keep the shield going long enough to protect herself *and* summon a sword long enough to use it. Not at the same time, of course, but she would get there.

She could taste revenge. It was so close.

"Good!" Fyrn shouted.

The blast of light stopped, and she peeked over her shield to find Fyrn smirking a bit as he watched her. Styx applauded, squeaking loudly as he clapped.

She stood up straight, silently commanding the shield in her hand to get a little smaller so that she could hold it. It obeyed, shrinking ever so slightly, and her shoulder relaxed a bit in relief. She grinned. "How long until you think I'm ready?"

Fyrn shook his head. "Don't get cocky. Luak is much better than you."

"For now," she said, grinning.

He clicked his tongue, pinching the bridge of his nose. "You have way too much to learn to be thinking about revenge, Victoria. Focus on your studies, and revenge will come."

Her smile faded. Patience wasn't one of her strengths.

"Wait, what's that around your neck?" Fyrn pointed his staff at Victoria's chest.

She looked down to see the diamond amulet her parents had left her. "Oh, something I discovered at the bank. My parents left it for me."

"May I examine it?"

With a slight limp to her step from the training, Victoria crossed the distance between them and set it in his palm. He examined it, eyes crossing a little as he inspected the gemstone.

"Victoria, this is no trinket. It's a powerful object."

Her brows shot up her forehead. "Is it?"

He nodded and pointed to the dagger in her arm. "That is a Rhazdon Artifact, obviously, but there are other magical artifacts as well. Not all are filled with dark magic. Most are created for a single purpose, but they need to be powered by something. Think of artifacts as flashlights—they need batteries to work. In Oriceran, those batteries are called relics. Do you follow?"

"I think so," she said hesitantly.

"This diamond is both artifact and relic, meaning they're packaged together. You will never have to power this with your own magic. It will simply work for you, always."

"What does it do?"

"Ordinarily, I couldn't tell you what an artifact does without intense study and research. This one, however, I've seen before. It warns its owner of danger. You must wear it for it to work, but if you do, it will begin to glow if there's someone nearby who wishes to hurt you. I have no idea how your parents found it, though. Last I heard, it was lost."

Victoria chuckled. "That sounds like something they'd go after, no question."

He handed it back to her. "Keep that close. It's priceless."

Victoria smiled, studying the necklace with newfound admiration.

"Now, back to work. Again!" he said, lifting his staff and pointing the crystal toward her.

She hefted her shield to cover her face, willing it larger as she prepared for another onslaught. She didn't care what Fyrn said—she was getting better every day, learning to control her gifts more quickly than she had ever learned anything in her life. It was natural, like breathing.

She wouldn't have to wait long.

CHAPTER TWENTY-FIVE

As Victoria emerged from the training cave, the light from the crystals above dimmed to twilight, casting shadows across the ground. Fyrn still led the way, his staff tapping the ground as he led them back to his cottage to plan the next day's strategy.

Somewhere nearby, a soft and familiar sound tugged on Victoria's ear. She paused, craning her neck as she listened. It grew louder and louder, until she could finally recognize it.

Crying.

"Fyrn, wait," she said, taking a few steps toward the sound. She craned her ears again, and the noise became clearer. It sounded like a little girl sobbing.

"Victoria, what—"

She bolted toward the sound, not caring if Fyrn told her to ignore it. She ran through an immaculate street lined with lavish homes, and the crying grew louder with every step. As she passed the mansions' elaborate gardens filled with colorful succulents and mosses, her eyes scanned every yard as she tried to find the little girl who was crying.

Victoria rounded a corner in the road only to find a little goblin girl hunched over a body. The child cried, her ears flapping like wings, her hands covering her eyes. Between sobs, she mumbled something unintelligible.

Victoria knelt beside her, glancing fleetingly at the corpse on the ground. She did a double take when she recognized him—it was the grouchy goblin who sometimes visited Bertha's shop. She lifted the girl's chin, and sure enough, this was the little goblin who had given Victoria the flower all those weeks ago. With a flare of recognition in the girl's eyes, the little goblin wrapped her tiny arms as far as they would go around Victoria's waist.

The girl said something again, but it wasn't in a language Victoria could understand. She held the goblin close, studying the corpse on the ground. She didn't even know where to look for a pulse.

Green blood oozed from large gashes in his shoulder. From the crescent-moon pattern, it looked like the bite of a massive animal. The marks curved around his torso, his arm, his neck, even his face. His nose had been flattened, and his ears were still. From the looks of it, he wasn't breathing.

Victoria held the girl tighter and looked around, desperate to get her to safety and simultaneously in a panic to figure out what could have done something like this. It took a moment, but her eyes eventually settled on the entrance to a tunnel not unlike the one she and Fyrn used to get to their training cave.

She had a flashback to the slithering tail in the tunnels below, and her heart beat faster.

"This is bad," Fyrn said, kneeling beside her. In her panic, she hadn't even heard him approach.

"We have to get her to safety, and we have to tell the king about this attack," Victoria said, holding the girl in her arms as she stood.

"You're right," Fyrn said, frowning as he studied the entrance to the tunnel.

"What could do something like this?"

"I don't know." He studied her, pausing for a moment as their gazes met. His jaw tensed, and he stood a little taller.

Unbelievable. He was scared.

Victoria kept her eyes on the entrance to the tunnel as she slowly backed away. She cradled the girl's head against her shoulder, doing her best to block the child's view of the dead body.

"It's going to be okay," she lied.

———

Audrey sat at one of the chairs in Bertha's kitchen, staring at her fingers as she tapped the wooden surface of the table. Victoria sat across from her, and Bertha stood in the corner. No one spoke. No one knew what to say.

Bertha began to pace, the floor creaking with every thump of her heavy feet. "Could it have been an attack by a fellow citizen?"

"Not unless that person has swords for teeth and a jaw as wide as a door." Victoria tugged the ends of her hair, wrapping the locks around her fingers, a dead giveaway that she was nervous.

"Who was the victim?" Audrey asked.

Bertha wiped away a tear. "A prominent investor in the city. He might've been grumpy and unpleasant, but he changed hundreds of lives for the better by developing previously uninhabitable areas and creating homes for citizens who didn't have one. He was loved, and there will be hell to pay when we discover who did this."

"What about the girl?" Victoria asked softly.

"Last I heard, she was with her mother."

"Good," Victoria said softly.

Audrey rubbed her temples. She couldn't imagine what it was like to find someone's corpse. For the moment, she didn't envy Victoria at all.

"We have to find and kill whatever did this," Victoria said, eyes locking with Audrey's.

Audrey shook her head. "Victoria, we have enough on our plates. Don't make this our problem."

"Of course it's our problem!"

Audrey gritted her teeth. She frowned and narrowed her eyes, saying everything she needed to without uttering a word. *Stop playing hero.*

Victoria huffed and crossed her arms, leaning back. *I'm not!*

Audrey rolled her eyes and tapped on her left index finger against her right wrist. *You can't even control the Rhazdon Artifact. Don't expose yourself.*

"Yes, I can!" Victoria snapped, hitting her fist on the table.

Bertha jumped. "What?"

"I can control it," Victoria said, ignoring Bertha as she glared at Audrey.

"You're going to go gallivanting off into the wilderness with a few powers you are only just beginning to understand to kill something the size of a house? Are you insane?"

"Powers?" Bertha quirked an eyebrow.

"You haven't been watching my training. You haven't seen what I'm capable of."

"This isn't our problem!"

Victoria pointed to the back of the house, through the glass doors that led to Bertha's little yard. "If the city is in danger, we all are! Fairhaven isn't that big, Audrey. Besides, if we can help, it's our job to try!"

Audrey set her palms on the table, sighing as something clicked for her. This would hurt to say, but Victoria needed to hear it. "Playing hero won't bring your parents back. It won't make them proud. It won't make everything you've endured so far worth it."

"How dare you—"

"I'm serious," Audrey interrupted. "You'll expose yourself. One swing, and everyone in this town will know what you are."

Bertha crossed her arms. "For goodness sake, what the hell are you two talking about?"

Victoria backed away from the table, running her hands through her hair as she paced the kitchen. For several minutes, no one spoke. Audrey watched Victoria's every step, waiting for her friend to make a stupid decision or run into the street, swinging a sword made of dark magic and brass for all to see.

And Bertha, bless her, seemed to be waiting for something to make sense.

"It's risky," Victoria eventually said.

"It's stupid," Audrey corrected.

"It's not." Victoria glared at her, and Audrey looked away. She couldn't hold Victoria's eye when she scowled like that.

"That's it? Your life for the city?" Audrey asked softly.

"We should at least look for the creature. Find its cave. Identify its weaknesses."

"I know you better than that. You'll go after it."

"We would be in the caves. Who cares? No one goes down there."

"Plenty of people go down there. And if someone sees you fighting it?" Audrey dragged her finger over her throat in the universal sign for *dead meat.*

"We don't know they'll think that way."

Audrey scoffed. "Don't be ridiculous. It's a death sentence."

"I've had about enough of this cryptic bullshit," Bertha snapped.

Audrey didn't flinch, and to her credit neither did Victoria. Bertha fumed. Her cheeks had turned red, almost black, and her glowering eyes shifted from Audrey to Victoria and back.

"I'm sure they have an army, V. They don't need us," Audrey said.

"Maybe not, but if I have to choose between saving myself and someone else, you know what choice I'll make." Victoria pushed away from the table and stormed into the shop, most likely to cool off in the street outside.

Bertha turned the full force of her frustration on Audrey. "Little one, you had better—"

"I'm sorry, Bertha. The moment I can, I'll explain everything. Thank you for the drink." She drained the last of her cup and offered a subtle bow of respect to her mentor and friend before following Victoria outside.

Audrey knew full well what choice her friend would make, and it would probably end in blood.

CHAPTER TWENTY-SIX

Luak sat in the king's private office, his feet on the monarch's desk even though he sat in the guest chair. The king, coward that he was, didn't say a thing. He merely leaned against the window, staring through the glass at the magnificent city below.

"Pity about that investor," Luak said. It took all of his energy to suppress a wicked grin.

The king frowned.

"It seems as though your plan to keep the beast a secret has backfired," Luak continued.

The king shook his head. "It was contained."

Luak clicked his tongue in disappointment. "I'm worried for you, my king. There's dissent, talk that you are too weak to protect your people. I fear for you," he lied for effect. "What's worse is that I hear you now have a Rhazdon host in your city."

The king froze, not breathing. "You're lying."

"I wish I was, my liege."

"What do you know of this host?"

"Not much," Luak lied again. "But for you, I can find out more."

"Do."

Even from here, Luak could see the king's hands trembling. He crossed his arms, no doubt in an effort to hide it, but it was clear: King Bornt was nervous. Weak as he was, he should have been running for the hills. The wizard monarch had no idea what Luak had in store for him if he stayed.

"I have a proposition for you," Luak said.

The king nodded without looking at him. "I assumed as much. You always do."

"You'll want to hear this one."

"Out with it."

"I will kill the monster. I will soothe the dissent in the city, and ensure that everyone here loves you and gives you credit for killing the beast. Not another soul will die, and you will keep your throne."

This got the king's attention. He leaned against the wall, his full attention now focused on Luak. "And in return?"

"You become a figurehead with no power. I rule Fairhaven. I make the laws. The city adores you, and you continue to live here, but you hand me the keys."

"Get out," the king said, seething.

Luak chuckled and stood, but he crossed the gap between them instead of heading for the door. He leaned in, his nose barely an inch from the king's as he towered over him. "Your people think you are weak because you are. It's only a matter of time before you lose the crown. Think about my proposition. It's the only way for you to cling to the last shreds of your power."

With that, Luak left at a slow and steady pace, letting the door swing gently shut behind him. He adjusted his collar, wondering how he could rile up the creature he had planted in the tunnels. A single killing wasn't enough. It must not have been hungry, but he could fix that.

A few more well-placed rumors about the king hiding the truth and a few more deaths—perhaps a whole family enjoying a day out together—would be enough to start a riot big enough to overthrow the king.

And of course, Luak thought with a wicked grin, the movement would need a leader.

CHAPTER TWENTY-SEVEN

Victoria paced the cobblestones in front of Bertha's shop, arms crossed as she scanned the empty street. This was the first time she had ever seen Main Street almost completely empty. Usually there were so many heads bobbing down the street that it was difficult to tell the bodies from each other, but today everyone was staying indoors.

"There is a curfew now, apparently," Audrey said, the door shutting behind her.

"What did you tell Bertha?"

Audrey frowned, grimacing a little in an expression that Victoria had long ago learned meant, *C'mon, really?*

Victoria shrugged. "If anyone should be told, it's her."

"I wouldn't want to put her in that position," Audrey said, hands on her hips.

"To choose?"

Audrey nodded. "She would have to choose between her city and two strangers she took into her home."

"You think she would turn us in?"

Audrey grinned, shaking her head a little bit. "I know she wouldn't. That's the problem."

Victoria laughed. "It's nice to have at least one person on our side."

"Two, if you count Fyrn."

Victoria nodded. "I do."

"Now that you've had some time to cool off, what do you think of your little plan to go after this creature?"

Victoria frowned, eyeing Audrey. "Don't talk down to me."

Audrey lifted her hands in surrender. "I'm absolutely positive this city has an army. I think you should leave the fighting to the pros while you and I learn about the city. I mean, think about it—we didn't even know how long our money would last a couple of days ago, and now you want to hunt something that can create wounds like the ones on that poor goblin's body? It killed him, Victoria. It won't hesitate to kill us, too."

"Nor would it hesitate to kill anyone else," Victoria added.

Audrey's shoulders drooped a bit. "I know. I know you're strong, Victoria. And I know you have these newfound gifts you're learning to control. You're capable, but I don't want you to bite off more than you can chew right now, that's all."

"I know my limits."

Audrey caught her eye, brow quirking a bit. "Do you?"

Victoria hesitated, scanning Audrey's face as something clicked in the back of her mind. "You're scared I'm going to die."

As if Victoria's words had flipped a switch, tears burned

in Audrey's eyes. She swallowed hard, staring at the rooftops for a few moments. When she did finally speak, her words came out in a whisper. "Of course I am."

"You're scared I'm going to be reckless and get myself killed."

"Y-yes. Yes, okay? Yes!"

Victoria nodded. This confirmed a deep fear she'd had since she first came to Fairhaven. She paced a bit, trying to figure out how to word what she wanted to say next. "When you came down here with me, when you joined me, you knew I was on the warpath. This isn't a field trip. It never was. You knew this was about revenge for me. You knew this was about blood and sweat and vengeance. If I die, Audrey, it will be for a purpose."

"But killing this monster doesn't help you get vengeance."

"You're right."

"Then why do any of this? Why care? It sucks that the girl lost her dad, but come on, Victoria. Keep your eye on the big picture!"

The words wounded Victoria like a punch to the gut, but they disappointed her more than anything. "What's gotten into you?"

"Into *me*? What's gotten into *you*?"

"Audrey, we've been friends forever. You were willing to come here with me, abandon your life to help me get revenge and seek justice for my parents. Hell, you even fired a gun in the bank parking lot to protect me. I love you like a sister, and I always will. But *fuck*, woman! How can you be so heartless as to say this girl doesn't matter? That these people don't matter? Don't you love Fairhaven?"

Audrey frowned but didn't answer.

Victoria pressed it. "This place is magical and fucked up and beautiful, and I never want to leave. I don't understand it and probably never will, but we can't leave these people to die, Audrey. You've heard the rumors about this king. He doesn't care about the people. He doesn't care about keeping them alive, keeping them safe, or even keeping them happy. The people here are on their own more and more, and the Army doesn't serve them. The Army serves him. And what will happen if he locks himself in his palace? If he pretends this doesn't exist and that there's not a problem? Audrey, I'm not saying we have to fight, but we need to be prepared to if that's what it takes."

An indent appeared in Audrey's cheek where she was almost certainly biting it to stem the flood of words she would probably regret. Victoria had learned a long time ago not to push Audrey to share what was on her mind. Audrey would share if she wanted to.

Victoria put her hands on Audrey's shoulders. "This is as much about justice as revenge, Audrey. I have to do this. Are you with me?"

Audrey's lip curled in the subtlest of smiles. "To the end, you friggin' idiot."

Victoria and Audrey had a deal: they would scope out the tunnels during the day to see if they could get more info on the creature, and at night they would strategize. When they encountered the creature that had killed the goblin, Victoria would attack only if she had no other choice.

In the meantime, they would play a bit of Berserk.

Wearing the silver jersey of their team, Victoria shook out her hands and hopped up and down to get her blood going. She stood in the center of the field, scanning the massive stadium. Above her, the audience roared. The field was covered with players of all shapes and sizes, silver jerseys against black.

A horn blew long and loud—the warning bell, telling everyone that the game would start soon. Tense, ready to go, and a little bit nervous, Victoria jogged over to Audrey. A goblin in a black and white referee's shirt dragged a net filled with the indestructible fidgets, who rolled against the bag as if more eager to get onto the field than the players.

Her team lined up as the referee took center field, hand raised to quiet the din. His voice boomed over the stadium, impossibly loud. "Ladies and gentlemen, creatures of all ages, I welcome you to the Berserk Seasonal Kickoff! As a reminder to our players, our most important rule is, no magic! Aside from that, your only job is to win."

The crowd roared, and he spoke in another language Victoria didn't recognize. Maybe he was cycling through the most common ones so that as many as possible could understand him.

As he spoke, she surveyed her team. Seven ogres and three elves, plus her and Audrey. Not only were they the only humans, but they were the only girls.

Time to represent.

The opposing team seemed to be comprised entirely of ogres lined up shoulder to shoulder, all but foaming at the mouth to begin. They thumped their chests, roared, and jostled each other as they prepared to charge. If one of them plowed into her, she might not wake up for a few days.

Fun.

In the final seconds before the starting bell, she scanned the guest box for Fyrn's trademark staff. He hated crowds, so she doubted he would have come. Still, deep in her heart, she had hoped he would anyway. There were elves she didn't recognize, and Bertha waved with a mighty smile from the top row of seats. Victoria waved back.

A familiar and utterly ridiculous hat appeared, and bit by bit, Fyrn's beard and staff came into view. He nodded once to her and went to find a seat.

She grinned. He had come after all.

The starting horn blew. With a flourish, the referee tossed the net of fidgets onto the mossy ground and disappeared into thin air. The crowd roared. Hundreds of feet smacked the bleachers like thunder.

Both teams charged the field, everyone aiming either for one of the fidgets or for an opponent. After all, if an opponent threw in the towel and went to the wizard medic, he would be out for the rest of the game. Better to get an early lead. Two ogres rammed each other, and the ground rumbled beneath them.

An elf ran straight for Victoria, but she dodged him effortlessly. As if on cue, Edgar tackled the elf, giving her time to bolt ahead and find one of the fidgets. Even though they weren't supposed to use magic, she didn't consider her newly learned stealth and speed as breaking the rules. Light as a feather, she bolted across the field, scanning the grass for the telltale golden eyes of one of the green fidgets. No green, but she did spot a black one. Chasing after it, she plucked the little critter off the ground and ran toward their opponents' goal.

"Oi!" someone shouted.

Edgar ran alongside her, the ground rumbling under his footsteps. He gestured to the fidget in Victoria's hands.

Oh, thank goodness. She did *not* want to be the one to pummel through the opponent's three goalies. She tossed him the creature, which he caught easily. He tore ahead, about to score fifty points for the Plits.

Victoria skidded to a halt, a broad smile on her face as she prepared for her second catch of the day. A green one. She really, *really* wanted to catch a green one in her first game.

Someone screamed.

At first Victoria thought someone in the audience had gotten carried away, but the second scream chilled her to the bone. It was bloodcurdling, the sound someone makes when they get stabbed. She paused and surveyed the audience, some of whom are starting to look around, too. A few sections of the higher bleachers began to evacuate, heads bobbing as people pushed their way out of the stadium.

Her breath caught in her throat as more and more of the spectators began to funnel out the stadium. One by one the players on the field slowed and looked up as well, but no one seemed to know what was happening.

Deep in her gut, Victoria knew something was very, very wrong. She looked at Audrey, who nodded.

Game over.

They raced toward the exit together without a word shared between them. After a moment's hesitation, many of the players on her side followed suit, ground trembling as even the teams evacuated.

While many of the players retreated to the locker rooms, Victoria headed straight for the street. She needed to know what was happening, but in her gut she had the feeling she already knew.

Before they could reach the street outside, something roared. The grating screech was like nails on a chalkboard, and every fiber of Victoria's being cringed. She forced herself forward, tensing her arms as she prepared to use her dark magic if necessary.

Heels kicking up dust as she ran, she passed every type of creature she had ever seen in Fairhaven. Ogres, elves, gremlins, goblins—everyone ran in different directions. It was chaos. People screamed. Doors slammed. Glass shattered. But so far, Victoria couldn't figure out what they were running from.

Whatever it was, it roared again, and Victoria raced toward the sound with Audrey in tow.

They rounded the corner of the stadium to find a massive creature in the street with several bodies littered around it. It roared a third time, teeth protruding from its mouth like fangs, claws reaching for any creature who came near it.

"Holy shit, it's a snarx," Audrey said under her breath.

True to Bertha's word, it really did look like the ugly lovechild of a basilisk and a massive centipede. It screamed, and the windows in a house across from the stadium burst.

"Yay," Victoria said, tensing. Her breath came in short

bursts as she sized up the monster, trying to figure out a game plan.

"Victoria, wait," Audrey grabbed her arm.

"We don't have time—"

"The only way we have a chance against this is if you use your, uh, *thing*. But we're exposed out here. Even if you kill it, even if you save them, they'll be afraid of you. They'll probably kill you. Even if we can escape, you won't have Fairhaven anymore. You'll lose everything."

Victoria grabbed both of Audrey's elbows, leaning her forehead against her friend's. "According to Fyrn, no host has ever saved someone before. Maybe I can change the stigma, Audrey. I can show them there's nothing to fear. Am I scared? Hell yeah, but when has that ever stopped me? It's wrong to let the people in this city die because I'm afraid."

"Oh, you'll definitely die," Shiloh said with a sigh, suddenly beside them.

Victoria flinched, grimacing. "Thanks, Shiloh. Good pep talk."

Audrey sucked in a deep breath, nodding. At this point in their friendship, Audrey should know better than to try to change Victoria's mind about something she cared this deeply about.

Audrey offered her fist. "To the end?"

Victoria grinned, bumping her fist against Audrey's. "To the end."

The creature snarled, its tail crashing into the stadium wall. Blocks of stone hurtled to the ground, coming within inches of crushing pedestrians who were still trying to get away from the monster.

"What's the plan?" Audrey asked.

Victoria was looking around, mind buzzing as she formulated a strategy, when she saw a familiar tunnel not far away. She and Fyrn had used it once or twice to get to their training cave, to shake off anyone who might have been following them.

"Get it away from everyone else!" she shouted.

Victoria charged, waving her hands to get the beast's attention. Beside her, Audrey followed suit. The creature zeroed in on them, its front legs crashing to the ground. The ground shook underneath it. Victoria lost her balance for a second and stumbled and the snarx charged, immensely faster than it should have been. Victoria recovered her balance and raced toward the tunnel.

Side by side, she and Audrey ran as fast as they could. The beast would snap at them now and then. It missed Audrey by inches. As she ducked the attack, she fell, rolling. Dust kicked into the air. She regained her balance and jumped into an alley seconds before the creature's tail flattened her.

"*Audrey!*"

"Go! I'll get my sword and follow!"

Victoria bolted, heels almost kicking her butt as she ran with everything she had. The monster snapped, its saliva splattering her hair.

It was close. Too close.

The snarx roared. Adrenaline, panic, and a little bit of regret blended together in a raging cocktail that fueled Victoria. She just had to make it to the tunnel, and then she could draw her weapon. Just a little bit farther.

A searing pain ripped down her back. She screamed

and fell, rolling. The rough cobblestone bit into her arms and shoulders, bruising her. Her sleeve caught on a loose shard of metal embedded in a chunk of debris.

The fabric ripped, exposing her entire right arm.

Though most of the street was empty, many were watching from the buildings. She could hear them gasp through the broken windows, and looked down to find her Rhazdon Artifact completely revealed. The smooth metal and rubies glistened in the light from the crystals overhead.

Her secret was out. No reason not to use it.

She summoned her sword, focusing her attention on making the tip as sharp as possible. The creature neared, something in its throat clicking like a rollercoaster car on its initial ascent as it raised its head to strike.

It bared its teeth and dove for her, and she swung her sword. The blade sliced off a bit of its tongue, and blood spurted into the air. Anything it hit sizzled, as though the blood were acid, and Victoria was careful to duck and roll out of the way. The beast screamed, striking at her with its tail, and she dodged again with only a second to spare.

She had to get it out of the city.

"Victoria!"

Only fifty feet away, Audrey waved. She had a sword of her own now, and pointed it toward the tunnel. Victoria nodded and raced toward the entrance, shoulders aching and legs throbbing. It didn't matter how much pain she was in—she had to get this thing away from the people it was actively trying to kill.

She just hoped it didn't kill her in the process.

CHAPTER TWENTY-EIGHT

Standing on one of the balconies in the palace, Luak couldn't believe his luck.

Below him, a small war waged between the Rhazdon host he wanted dead and the monster he had smuggled into the city's caves. For the most part his monster was winning—or it had been until the girl revealed herself.

But this was perfect.

He didn't care about the creature, since his plan from the beginning had been to kill it and become the town's hero. But now she had shown herself to be a Rhazdon host. That meant he would not only save the city from the terrible monster lurking in its depths, but also from the Rhazdon host their king had so foolishly allowed into their midst.

Luak grinned, popping his collar as he retreated into the guest suite. In a few moments he would race to the city's rescue, and incidentally retrieve the Rhazdon Artifact which was rightfully his.

CHAPTER TWENTY-NINE

Victoria raced into the tunnels, the glow of the thousands of crystals embedded within the rock whizzing by like tiny green blurs in her peripheral vision. The creature's body banged against the rock, loosing a torrent of pebbles from the ceiling.

It took everything in her to remember the way while being chased by a creature that wanted to eat her alive.

Right. Left. Left. Left. Shit, no, other left.

She raced through the tunnels, desperately hoping she could remember the correct path. She and Fyrn didn't come this way often, and she wasn't usually in a state of panic when they did.

Phase One of her spur-of-the-moment strategy had worked: get the beast away from the city. Phase Two would be trickier. The fact of the matter was that she couldn't fight the beast in the tunnel; there simply wasn't enough space, and it would pin her easily. She wouldn't be able to run or dodge or duck as she preferred to do in a fight. She desperately needed to find that cave and its meadow, and she needed to do it soon. Hopefully Audrey had kept up with them and was still on the beast's tail because she could certainly use the help.

As she rounded the bend, light streamed from a familiar source. She grinned. Thank goodness. She had found it.

Shoes squishing a bit on the soft mossy ground, she sprinted into the purple meadow grass as the crash of the waterfall almost drowning out the monster's thundering footsteps. It roared again, the sound echoing in the cavern, and she skidded on her heels.

It snapped at her, but she jumped out of the way. The wounds on her arms and back still bled heavily since she was focusing all her attention on her sword, but that was fine. They weren't bad enough for her to wish away the sword yet.

She scanned the beast's head, neck, and underbelly—the stereotypical weak spots. Since she had never fought this kind of creature before, her weak understanding of Dungeons & Dragons was all she could draw on to defeat it.

No way *that* would fail.

Okay, time to focus. She hesitated, hair on her arms standing on end as her body buzzed with fear and anticipation.

Step one: get rid of that damn tail.

The creature's tail flailed around the cavern, breaking crystals as it pummeled the walls and kicked up a heavy spray of mist any time it smacked the lake. She kept her distance, looking for a pattern to the tail's movement. When it curled around the beast again, ready to strike at her, she took the opportunity to attack. Sword raised high and with all her strength, she swung the blade and it bit deep into the base of the tail. The flesh gave beneath her sword like butter, and her blade clanged against the rock beneath it. The monster screamed, blood spraying against the wall. It bared its teeth, hissing, and she suddenly had a great view of its neck.

One more blow should end this.

Victoria seized the opportunity, lifting her sword over her head and jumping, blade aimed for the creature's exposed throat. She swung with all her might, her sword getting bigger and growing heavier as she leapt through the air. Her Rhazdon Artifact must have been tapping into her deep desire to kill this thing, but *damn* was it getting heavy.

Because of the added weight, she missed her mark. The blade sank into the creature's shoulder, embedded deeply, and for a second she hung there, unable to wrest her sword loose. The snarx screamed and turned on her, teeth bared to strike. The sword wouldn't budge.

Victoria quelled the rising panic with a deep breath and a plan: she focused all her energy on healing her wounds. Her attention shifted from the sword, and it disappeared on cue. She dropped to her feet seconds before the creature lunged.

"Victoria!" Audrey shouted. She stood by the entrance, sword raised and ready.

"Let's try that again!" Victoria said.

Audrey nodded and rolled out of the way as the creature lunged toward her, then swung for its throat. A slit appeared in the flesh as a river of blood shot out.

The monster screeched, tongue flickering in and out as

it stared down at Audrey. And though she hadn't intended to use her friend as bait, by happy accident the creature's neck was now completely vulnerable.

With all her energy and all her might, Victoria prepared to attack again. She lifted her sword over her head, her eyes zeroing in on the wound Audrey had made at the base of its throat. She willed her sword to be as sharp as possible, and the reflection of the light off her blade hit the wall in front of her.

As the creature screamed one more time, she swung.

CHAPTER THIRTY

F yrn hadn't felt this anxious in years.

He stood on the road nearest the royal balcony, where the king surveyed and tried to calm the mob that had descended upon the palace after the creature's attack. Twenty were dead, but it would have been far worse if not for the Rhazdon host who had also descended upon their city.

Granted, no one knew quite what to make of the situation. No one had heard of a Rhazdon host helping a city before, much less saving its people from a monster's attack. Feelings in the crowd ranged from panic to fear, neither of which boded well for Victoria. He had to do something, smooth this all over somehow.

Too bad he was a shit public speaker.

On the balcony, Luak leaned toward the king. Fyrn grimaced. He had to hear what those two were saying.

He tapped his staff twice on the ground, focusing his magic and muttering a few words under his breath. A ringing sounded in his ear, and he pointed his staff toward

Luak. Like a radio settling on a station, the elf's voice slowly faded in and out until it became clear.

"...but my offer still stands," Luak said.

"And you'll kill them both? The girl and the creature?"

"You have my word."

King Bornt seemed to wrestle with the thought, and Fyrn wondered what the price was. Luak had both wealth and influence, so there wasn't much he could want. Unfortunately, Fyrn didn't know the elf well enough to know the man's ambitions. Whatever was, it couldn't be good.

The king nodded. Luak smirked and disappeared through the open doorway. Fyrn tensed. Whatever had just happened, it was bad.

"It's the host!" someone said from the crowd.

For a brief moment, Fairhaven was silent. No one spoke. No one moved. No one even breathed. Every citizen present focused his or her attention on the tunnel into which Victoria, Audrey, and the monster had disappeared.

Victoria emerged from the shadows, nothing but a silhouette at first, but the light slowly illuminated the features of her face and the blood smeared across her cheek. She and Audrey dragged something behind them, grimacing as they struggled.

The creature's head.

As they neared the crowd, Victoria slowed and surveyed them. She carried neither the sword nor the shield, likely because she had to focus all her attention on dragging the monster.

In that moment, it clicked for Fyrn. This had been Luak, all of it. He had set up the creature to force the king to accept his proposition, and had perhaps even set up Victoria to expose herself.

Fyrn had to get to Victoria. This could all implode and everything, including the powerful young woman he had helped to create, would be destroyed.

Victoria stood by the entrance to the cave, poised to run if she had to.

Truthfully, she didn't want to. She was tired of hiding, tired of being afraid to share what she really was. This was a city filled with ogres and gremlins. Surely if they could accept each other, they could accept her.

A single person buried deep within the crowd began to clap. It was slow at first, almost silent, but it was joined by another, and another, and another until the entire audience erupted into applause. The mob cheered, and some even approached her with smiles on their faces.

On the palace balcony overlooking the road, several men and a few women huddled together, heads leaning in as if quietly discussing something. One, a man, wore a gilded crown. Beside him stood Diesel, and she grimaced a little inside. But even that pompous wizard clapped for her. In fact, the only one not applauding was the king.

The king snapped his fingers, and Victoria's stomach churned. Though she had been standing on the ground a moment before, she now knelt before him, about to be sick.

"Nonsense, no need to bow." Diesel gently grabbed her

arm and helped her to her feet, apparently not under-standing why she had knelt in the first place.

As her nausea faded, she was able to meet the king's gaze. He glared. He watched her as if he was waiting for her to attack, and his face twitched ever so slightly. It was almost as though he was afraid.

Victoria frowned, but the king grabbed her wrist and lifted it into the air, presenting her to his subjects. "I give you the Hero of Fairhaven!"

The crowd roared louder. Victoria smiled, grateful. She might have been covered in blood and bruises, but at least she didn't have to hide anymore.

The king leaned in, his mouth by her ear. "If you ever threaten my control over the city, you will be dead before you can do anything of note."

She glared at him over the shoulder of her raised arm. If she were in his position, she would have been more concerned with the people in her city than her power over it. "I have no intention of stealing your crown."

He pursed his lips and returned his attention to the crowd, forcing a smile where there had been a grimace a second before.

"She's no hero!" a man shouted from behind her.

Victoria spun on her heels, the familiar voice like slime in her ear. Sure enough, Luak stood behind her, only a few feet separating them.

On impulse, Victoria summoned her sword.

The crowd and everyone on the platform gasped. All backed away except Diesel, who grinned. "Now that, my love, was incredibly attractive."

"Enough." Luak shoved the wizard aside and stalked

toward her. Victoria settled into her stance, her energy focused on sharpening her sword. It polished itself, gleaming like a lighthouse in the glow of the crystals above.

Luak pointed a long finger at her. "She's a Rhazdon host. She carries illegal dark magic within her. By law, she must be destroyed."

"She is pardoned," the king said with a smirk.

Luak glared at the monarch. "That's illegal."

Though the king didn't meet Luak's eyes, his voice remained firm. "It seems our host is unique. She did what even you could not do. Thus, she has been pardoned, and you are dismissed."

Luak bristled. "You cannot dismiss me."

"He just did," Victoria said.

Luak's eyes narrowed, and his hands clenched. A sharp crack filled the air. Victoria flinched, but she didn't dare look away from the man who had murdered her parents. He, however, shifted his gaze over her shoulder.

"Victoria," a familiar voice said softly in her ear.

She tilted her head to see Fyrn standing behind her. He set a hand on her shoulder. Audrey also stood on the balcony, blood on her face as she glared at Luak.

"Not now, Fyrn," she muttered.

"Listen to me," he insisted.

"Not—"

He leaned in, his voice so quiet she could barely hear him. "I beg you to listen to me. If you had asked me if you should attack the creature, I would have told you that you were ready. I would have encouraged you to try. You are not, however, ready to face him. He let that monster loose on the city. I believe he has been trying to control

Fairhaven, and you stopped him. Savor that victory. He can't attack you here without the Army killing him, but if you attack first, no one will stop him from ripping you to shreds in self-defense. You *will* be stronger than him. You *will* kill him, but not today."

Her grip on her sword tightened, and she glared at Luak as she processed what Fyrn had said. Frustrated, she finally shook her head and wished the sword away.

Luak frowned, a look of utter disgust crossing his face. He had lost, and he knew it. He stormed into the hallway behind the balcony and disappeared into the castle.

Soon she would shove her sword through his gut. Soon she would have justice. But for now, she had freed Fairhaven from his control.

She turned to face the crowd gathered below. They cheered, some of them screaming her name. She raised her right hand to wave, the Rhazdon Artifact glimmering in Fairhaven's crystalline light.

Luak couldn't escape justice for long. Victoria would have her revenge, and she would personally see that he paid for everything he had done.

Victoria & Audrey return in Shimmer (Fairhaven Chronicles #2), available now.

Oriceran is rife with secrets... and you may not want to know the answers.

Thanks to an ancient artifact, Victoria Brie is stuck with dark magic in her blood until the day she dies. And if she's not careful, that day will come too soon.

There are those who would kill her simply for what she is: a Rhazdon host, master of incredible power. To make matters worse, the madman who murdered her parents is dead-set on slitting her throat, too.

Like hell. Victoria won't go down without a fight.

But there's trouble brewing in the shadows of her beloved hometown. In the alleyways and shadows of the charmingly magical Fairhaven, dangerous magic from a bygone era is resurfacing. Worse still, it only reacts to the touch of a single being: Audrey, Victoria's best friend. It begins to twist Audrey's mind, urging her to a faraway land the world thought was lost...

...Atlantis.

There are answers in Atlantis, clues that could give Victoria the power to finally destroy the man who killed her parents. But every step she takes toward Atlantis shines light on a world brimming with lies, murder, and deception. If Victoria isn't careful, she'll lose Audrey to the mystical city buried beneath an ocean.

Victoria's used to being hunted... but *no one* threatens her friend and lives.

This series is an enchanting urban fantasy saga with sarcastic ogres, wise-cracking wizards, and a brutally addictive full-contact sport called Berserk. Your only regret will be not starting it sooner.

WARNING! This story contains cursing because these eighteen-year-olds are honorable rebels. If cursing offends you, you might not like this book.

AUTHOR NOTES - MARTHA CARR

DECEMBER 18, 2019

New decade, new year, new month and I recently turned 60. That can make meIt's been two and a half years since this series and the Oriceran Universe began and I get the unique opportunity to update the author notes with some hindsight. A rare gift. And it comes at the start of a new decade – 2020 – and for me as well. I've turned 60, which was an entirely different experience than expected. But more on that in a sec.

A lot has changed in that time. I've moved to a bigger house in Austin – the dream house (thank you Leira and troll, great Fans, and especially Michael).

But mostly what changed has changed is me. In order to handle actually getting to my destination I've had to change some of the views of myself. Frankly, I didn't see it coming. I thought this part would be a snap. Little did I know that it would take some inner adjustments.

This is the first time in my life I've known financial success. Even as a kid we were what the government calls food challenged. There was always enough but just barely.

Then I ended up spending most of my young adult life learning how to stretch a dollar, even while I pursued a career that I love as a journalist and author.

With the birth of the Oriceran Universe, which The Fairhaven Chronicles was an early part of, that's all changed. I had no idea how much my view of myself was tied to the idea of lack or loss or limits. I would still say I was an optimistic person but perhaps it was about the idea that things could get better or that I'd find a way to make things work. I never noticed that it wasn't about the idea that things will go well, be easy, be bountiful. And, once it was here settling into that idea was uncomfortable and has taken some time.

There's an old saying that in order to be successful I have to first believe I am capable of it – before it even shows up. That without that inner belief I'll make small decisions without even knowing it that can make it harder to become successful. There's that hindsight thing again and from my perch, two and a half years later – I can see a lot of those little places.

Then this small adjustment happened. When I met Michael Anderle I made the decision to say yes to whatever he had in mind without adding in my two cents worth. In other words, I decided to just trust and see where it took me. That made all the difference in the world. But there were more adjustments to come that took a bit more work.

I've had to reprogram the idea that if I can do it, I should be doing it and change it to – where is the best use of my time and skills. And, I've changed my 'dreaming of the future' from wondering what could go wrong to imagining what could go right and budgeting for just in case. Even that changes how I make decisions. Instead of protecting from I'm planning for something. It's taken some time and a willingness to just be uncomfortable on some days rather than do something short term to make me feel better about a dire future that probably wouldn't have happened.

Plus, it's easier to recognize opportunities when they arrive if that's what I've been picturing all along. Added bonus, what I really want – to maintain rather than expand – has become easier to see and even execute.

So, here we are at the beginning of things once again with a newer version of me. Can't wait to see what happens next. Thank you for coming along for the adventure and welcome to Oriceran where there are hundreds of stories. More adventures to follow.

look at things differently. I keep having the thought that if I haven't managed to change something by now, maybe I should make peace with it.

I mean how many decades do I keep trying to *fix* something before I realize the trying to fix it may be the problem. It's one of those things that I wish I had really understood better when I was a lot younger. And if I had it would have turned my outward search for what would make me fit better in the world, to an inward one of asking, what do I want?

What I want is to be happy with what is, instead of yearning for more or different like it's a necessity. In the past few years I've written as fast as I can, days, nights and weekends, holding down a full-time corporate job, and then moving and building a house, and the death of a sister. This past year I added on starting a universe on my own and trying to expand my business into other areas, while traveling far and wide at least once a month, sometimes more. I even held my old mini author convention in my house... twice.

I wasn't giving myself a chance to take a breath and absorb everything that happened, good and bad. There was no time.

Somewhere around the end of the year I knew I needed to make some changes. It was probably that impending end of one decade for both me and the planet and the start of another. And there's been something about 60 that's put things into a different perspective. What does all this running around add up to? I noticed I kept looking over at authors doing less work and more play or even just sitting still and wishing I was them.

Well, why can't I be them? I have choices. First one was to sell the new universe to LMBPN, pull all the books and reintroduce them, plus some new ones as the new Terranavis Universe. The relaunch started last week and already I feel lighter, happier. The next one was to stop planning business trips and just be here in the dream house for now with the dogs and get to know the neighbors. I made gingerbread cookies this Christmas and put my name, address and phone number and delivered them to everyone on my street. I started getting texts from everyone. It worked like a charm and I've even had a few over for dinner already.

I've also been getting up early and heading to the gym – one day at a time. Even yoga has seemed tough, but the bar is low – it can only get better. That's the other thing that

I'm really getting these days. This body is a loaner I'll have to give back at some point and how I treat it will play a part in how long I get to use it and how much use I get out of it. That has really hit home lately.

But I don't need to do any of it perfectly, or as well as it seems someone else is doing, or even great every single day. I just have to try and occasionally ask myself, *is this still what you want?* And then adapt, change and head out again. Happy New Year Everyone! More adventures to follow.

OTHER SERIES IN THE ORICERAN
UNIVERSE:

THE DANIEL CODEX SERIES
I FEAR NO EVIL
THE UNBELIEVABLE MR. BROWNSTONE
ALISON BROWNSTONE
SCHOOL OF NECESSARY MAGIC
SCHOOL OF NECESSARY MAGIC: RAINE CAMPBELL
FEDERAL AGENTS OF MAGIC
SCIONS OF MAGIC
THE LEIRA CHRONICLES
REWRITING JUSTICE
THE KACY CHRONICLES
MIDWEST MAGIC CHRONICLES
SOUL STONE MAGE
THE FAIRHAVEN CHRONICLES

OTHER BOOKS BY JUDITH BERENS

CONNECT WITH THE AUTHORS

Martha Carr Social

Website:
http://www.marthacarr.com

Facebook:
https://www.facebook.com/groups/MarthaCarrFans/

https://www.facebook.com/terranavisuniverse/

Michael Anderle Social

Michael Anderle Social
Website:
http://www.lmbpn.com

Email List:
http://lmbpn.com/email/

Facebook
https://www.facebook.com/TheKurtherianGambitBooks/